THIS WONDERFUL THING

Books by Adam Baron

BOY UNDERWATER

YOU WON'T BELIEVE THIS

THIS WONDERFUL THING

This Wonderful Thing

ADAM BARON

HarperCollins *Children's Books*

First published in Great Britain by
HarperCollins *Children's Books* in 2021
HarperCollins *Children's Books*
is a division of HarperCollins*Publishers* Ltd,
1 London Bridge Street
London SE1 9GF

www.harpercollins.co.uk

HarperCollins*Publishers*
1st Floor, Watermarque Building, Ringsend Road
Dublin 4, Ireland

1

ISBN 978-0-00-826708-7

Adam Baron asserts the moral right to be identified
as the author of the work.
A CIP catalogue record for this title is available from the British Library.

Typeset in 11pt Sabon by Palimpsest Book Production Ltd,
Falkirk, Stirlingshire
Printed and bound in England by CPI Group (UK) Ltd,
Croydon CR0 4YY

A CIP catalogue record for this title is available from the British Library.

For Kate Higgins, without whom Jessica and Milly
would never have existed

CHAPTER ONE

Jessica

Here's something that will make you LAUGH.

Yesterday we went to this place called Cuckmere Haven (Mum, Dad, Milly, Benji and me) and we played Pooh Sticks.

What, not clutching your sides? Not rolling on the floor in fits of giggles? Well, get this.

We played Pooh Sticks with a REAL POO!

We did! Honest! The poo belonged to Benji, who suddenly needed one. Dad had left his potty in the car so Mum pulled his shorts down by this big stream. Once Benji had done it, the poo rolled down between his trainers, bounced down the bank and jumped into the water. It sank, came up and swirled round to the middle, which would have been quite funny on its own. But Milly had an idea, something I have to admit because she's bigger than me and, if I take the credit, she'll hit me. She grabbed a stick from beneath a bush, me not knowing what she was up to until she'd lobbed it in.

'Pooh Sticks!' she bellowed. 'Pooh Sticks! We're playing Pooh Sticks with poo!'

'And sticks!' I shouted, as I grabbed one too and bunged it in after. 'We're playing Pooh Sticks with poo and sticks!'

And we weren't the only ones. Mum said, 'Girls!' and, 'Stop that!', but Dad clearly didn't think that 'Girls' applied to him. He grabbed a stick and chucked it in as well, leaving Mum to tut, and wipe Benji's bum, as the three sticks (and poo) began to move. Now we'd done what most people do when they're playing Pooh Sticks – cheat. Milly had thrown her stick in front of the poo, I'd thrown my stick in front of hers, and Dad had thrown his in front of mine. But it did NOT matter. While our sticks turned in circles or got snagged on weed and reeds, the little brown ball from Benji's bottom overtook them all.

'Poo,' Milly shouted, jumping up and down on the bank, 'is really good at Pooh Sticks!'

'Not all poo, I shouldn't think,' Dad said. 'Good job it wasn't a Sticky Poo!'

And, if you're not laughing now, forget it.

Well, Benji wanted to know what the fuss was about so, once he was bum-wiped and dressed, Dad hoisted him on to his shoulders. We all ran along the bank, Mum still not that amused as Milly and I shouted, 'Go, sticks!' while Dad and Benji shouted, 'Go, poo!' (and some birdwatchers looked on in shock). Mum was even more embarrassed when all the sticks got jammed up on some stones and Milly (who had Crocs on) ran into the stream.

'What are you doing?!' Mum yelled. Milly had pulled her dress up and was holding it in place with her chin.

'I can't let him win!' Milly said (she's super competitive). 'Sticks are useless!'

But Mum bellowed so loud that Milly got out without doing her own poo and we had to watch Benji triumph, our sticks soon far behind as the poo (almost as if it knew it was in a race) sprinted on. It swept beneath a footbridge. It wobbled past a few ducks, which some other birdwatchers were looking at. It began to go so fast that we could hardly keep level,

Benji almost hoarse from shouting and Dad panting to keep up with Milly and me. Then the stream got wider: there was a beach up ahead. The water was shallower and the poo started to skip, hopping out of the water as it leapt over little stones and round small boulders. It was hard to see, then more so as the sun burst out and made the water all sparkly.

'We're going to lose the poo!' Milly shouted, urging me to go faster. We stumbled on, thinking it was gone forever, until Milly caught sight of it. She pulled me by the arm and we sped up, just in time to see the poo roll out of the stream and on to the beach in front of us.

We stared down at the poo in awe and with respect. It didn't even look tired.

'Olympic standard,' Dad said, puffing to a halt beside us, then coughing. He's been having some problems with his fitness recently. 'Olympic-standard poo.'

'Let's do it again!' Milly said. 'Let's go back, only the poo belongs to me this time!'

'You pick it up then,' I said and, because Milly wants to win stuff so much, I swear she would have. But Mum arrived, really cross now, hissing at Dad about being poorly recently and how he wasn't supposed to run, as she scrabbled around in her backpack. She pulled out a nappy bag, scooped the poo up and marched off towards a bin. Milly sighed, and I was disappointed too, turning back to see if any of the sticks had made it that far. Maybe I'd come second, or First Pooh Stick Made Of Stick Not Poo. When Milly realised what I was looking for, though, she spun round too, both of us shielding our eyes until the sun went in.

Which is when I saw it.

In the water.

My eyes just settled on it and I stared, blinking, sort of calm inside as if, for some reason, it had wanted me to find it.

Not a stick.

Or another poo.

No.

I saw the thing that would change our lives forever.

CHAPTER TWO

Cymbeline

Here's something you won't believe.

I, Cymbeline Igloo, am on the front page of EVERY newspaper in the country. I am also trending heavily on Twitter, Instagram and Facebook (though Mum won't let me look at those because of the Russians) and will feature later on something called *Newsnight* (though I'll be in bed). And it's not just me. Marcus Breen's on these things too, as well as Lance, Veronique, Billy, Daisy, Vi, Miss Phillips and Charles Dickens (our class goldfish). He's called that because Veronique got to name him after she was pulled out of Miss Phillips's bobble hat. Charles Dickens wrote novels 2,000 years ago, including *A Tale of Two Cities*, which Veronique was reading (she's super brainy). It begins like this:

'It was the best of times, it was the worst of times.'

And that's a coincidence because what happened to me is like that too, only the best times come last and the worst times are where I'm about to start. And they were REALLY worst, so prepare yourself.

I waited AGES for my dad that day.

And I mean AGES.

The Reception kids left first, as usual. I could see them from our classroom window, staggering into the playground like wind-up toys about to run out of clockwork. Once they'd all been collected, we were allowed to go, me grabbing my two bags and jumping down the stairs. I ran into the playground and looked around, desperate to find Dad. But Elizabeth Fisher was picked up first from our class. She goes diving on Fridays and has to get to Crystal Palace. Her mum's always out there like the next runner in a relay race.

But Dad would be next surely.

Only he wasn't.

Daisy and Vi left then (football). Danny Jones's dad arrived to get him and then lots of parents came at once, everyone pointing across the playground, getting the nod from Miss Phillips before dashing off. I kept looking, but Dad didn't come and soon the crowds of kids and parents began to shrink because, of course, all the other years were out there getting picked up too.

I began to get this thin, liquidy feeling, which got worse, then worse again as fewer and fewer parents came through the gate into the playground. And then no one turned up at all and suddenly it was weird: how could a place be so busy, so swarming with people, and then so totally and completely empty? And it was empty. All that was left in the playground were four jumpers, six schoolbags, a glove, another glove (from a different pair), a lunchbox, a pair of trainers, a mobile phone, a baby's bottle and me.

Miss Phillips looked down. '*Who's* picking you up today?'

'My dad,' I said.

'Right. You did tell me, of course you did. That heavy?'

She meant my weekend bag, which I was still holding, my schoolbag on my back. 'Not really. I mean, not for long.'

Miss Phillips smiled, then smiled again at Mr Ashe

and Mrs Cooper, who were walking over from the staffroom with cups of tea. Mrs Cooper gave Miss Phillips a sympathetic smile, then waved to me.

Miss Phillips said, 'And it's *this* weekend?'

'*Yes*,' I said.

'Well, how about I go into the office and give him a little ring?'

'Okay. You don't need to, though. He is coming.'

'Of course,' Miss Phillips said, but she led me over to the office anyway. She told me to wait outside and I did, wishing I could run into the ICT room and go on Friv or something. There are no after-school clubs on Fridays, though, so I just had to stand there, watching, as Mr Briggs came out with a big set of keys. He locked the back door of the school and then went round the playground, shaking his head as he picked up the jumpers, bags, the lunchbox, the pair of trainers, the two (different) gloves, the mobile phone and the bottle, which he dropped into the lost-property bin.

'Did you call?' I said, when Miss Phillips came back. She ruffled my hair.

'I couldn't get through so I left a message.'

'Then he'll be here soon. Probably some delays on the trains.'

And I carried on waiting for my dad. I stared out through the gates, up the road, as Miss Phillips asked me *again* if I was *certain* that it was *this* weekend. I nodded, a hot red flower blooming inside me, my face beginning to burn as I remembered telling her. I'd told everyone in fact. The WHOLE CLASS knew what I was doing that weekend. The hot red flower seemed to blend in with the liquidy feeling as I forced my eyes past the parked cars, willing my dad to appear, trying to force him to run round the corner, panting, carrying *his* bag, waving as he ran towards me. That would scrub the liquidy feeling right out, and the image was so clear that I could almost believe it was happening – and, when I saw a movement on the steps that lead down from Blackheath to our school, my heart leapt up like a powerball. At the same time, the sun came out and blinded me. I squinted and held up my hand, though when the sun went in again it wasn't my dad that I saw.

It was my mum. Miss Phillips must have rung her too.

She had her car keys in her hand and looked harassed, though her whole face softened when she saw me.

'Oh, Cymbeline,' she said, after Miss Phillips had opened the gate for her. 'I'm sorry. I'm so sorry. I've tried calling him, I have, but . . . Oh. I'm just so *very* sorry.'

'Doesn't matter,' I said, though it did matter, something that I knew, and she knew, and Miss Phillips knew too, but which I tried my best to hide. I waved goodbye to Miss Phillips and Mr Briggs, who locked the gate behind us. Mum held my hand as she led me up the steps.

'Are Charlton at home tomorrow?' she asked.

'I don't know.'

'Well, if they are, shall we go?'

I nodded and for a second I pictured the Valley, Jacky Chapman leading the team out on to the bright green grass as Mum and I jumped up and down. But then it wasn't the Valley I was seeing. And it wasn't Jacky Chapman. It was the Nou Camp in Barcelona, which I'd googled about fifty times in the last month. The greatest football stadium in the world. And I was looking at De Jong and Griezmann, Piqué and Alba, and I was looking at Lionel Messi. And it wasn't Mum beside me, jumping up and down and shouting.

It was Dad.

I blinked the image away. I asked if Lance could come and Mum said yes, stopping as she got to the car. She didn't want to get in, though. Instead, she looked around, the same hope on her face that I'd had. Then she told me to wait there. She ran back down the steps and I could see her at the bottom, staring up the road. She got out her phone and I watched her tap in some numbers, then listen, and then hiss to herself, before shoving it back in her bag.

'Come on,' she said, when she'd walked back up again. And she took my bags from me and loaded them into the boot.

CHAPTER THREE

Jessica

It was on the far side of the stream – wedged under a big bit of wood. And I swear it was *looking* at me. I forgot about the sticks (and the poo). I stepped forward, trying to keep my eyes on it as I picked my way across the water on some of the bigger stones. But Milly spotted me. She turned and followed my gaze. I sped up, but I wasn't fast enough – of course. *And* she had Crocs on. All I could do was watch as she splashed through the water, not even caring that she was soaking me.

'Hey!' I shouted. 'That's mine!'

But Milly didn't answer. Instead, she pushed the piece of wood aside and grabbed it. She shook it, drops of water fanning out into the stream. Then she squeezed it like a swimming costume before holding it out in front of her.

'Dad!' she cried. 'Look what I found!'

'YOU!?' I tried to get to Milly then, but the stones were too slippery. My left foot went in the stream and my trainer filled up. 'No WAY did you find it. I saw it *first*.'

'Who says?' Milly laughed, getting away from me, then running back on to the beach. 'Anyway, I've got it now. That means it's *mine*.'

'It doesn't!' I screamed, not caring any more, just running right through the water towards her. 'Dad, tell her!'

'Tell her what?' Mum said.

Mum was walking back from the bin. She looked down at my soaked feet, before raising her eyebrows at Dad. He shrugged so she turned to my lying thief of a sister instead.

'What's *that*?' Mum said.

And the answer is as weird as WEIRD. You see, it wasn't some amazing thing that Milly and I had raced each other for. It wasn't a brand-new pack of pens, which I would have loved, or a rugby ball, which Milly would have adored. It wasn't a ten-pound note or a bag of sweets, or the last Golden Ticket in the world.

No.

It was something small, and drenched, covered in mud and sand. Mum and Dad grimaced and Benji just said, 'Yuck!' And he was right. Even from where I was standing, it STANK. It must have been in the stream for ages. Most people would have been perfectly happy to leave it there.

But, for a reason I didn't understand yet, I wanted it.

And so did Milly.

But Mum – well, she had other ideas.

CHAPTER FOUR

Cymbeline

'Cym,' Mum said, when we were both sitting in the car. 'There's really only one thing you can do when something like this happens.'

'Is there?' I said, not sure there was anything you could do. What could make up for not going to Barcelona with my dad when I'd been thinking about it for ages? I'd had my bag packed for weeks, and last night I'd been so excited that I hadn't been able to sleep. I kept checking the alarm clock to see if it was time to get up yet.

'Yes,' Mum said. 'And, while it won't change anything, it might make you feel better.'

'What is it then?'

'Go for ice cream,' Mum said. 'And lots of it.'

She pulled away and, instead of turning round towards home, she drove into Blackheath Village and parked. I thought she was taking me to the ice-cream van that's outside the church sometimes. Instead, we went to the posh place at the top where I stared at all the flavours, finally opting for blueberry and raspberry (Barcelona's colours). I was expecting a cone – but Mum frowned.

'I said *lots* of ice cream, didn't I?'

Mum ordered a whole tubful (mixed flavour) and we found a bench on the heath, using Mum's bamboo cutlery set because she didn't want to use plastic spoons. Mum is no-plastic OBSESSED these days, which of course I approve of – but it can be quite difficult. We go to this no-packaging shop where you take your own bottles and jars to refill. Mum's never got the right ones and, last week, when we were making flapjacks, she squirted shampoo in because it was in a golden-syrup bottle. The next morning I poured lentils into my cereal bowl and put cornflakes in the bird feeder. And later, in the bath, Mum squeezed tomato ketchup on my head.

It was organic, though.

Despite these 'teething problems', as Mum calls

them, I'm totally behind it. There's plastic everywhere. We went to Margate at half term and the beach was covered, from little pieces we made a mosaic out of to big drinks bottles. I even found a toy soldier in the seaweed, separated from his platoon. I played with him all day, wondering who'd lost him. I wished I could give him back because maybe he was really special to the owner. And maybe the kid was feeling something like I was at that moment.

Which, in spite of ice cream (though thanks, Mum), was still terrible.

'Mum?' I said, when the tub was all gone. 'Dad's an actor, isn't he?' Mum nodded. 'Which means he's always pretending. So do you think . . . ?'

'Yes, love?'

'That he was *ever* going to take me. I mean, *really*?'

Mum took a deep breath and turned away for a second. But then she shrugged. She hugged me and checked the back of the empty ice-cream tub for the recycling sign. She wasn't sure it could be recycled, but we decided to take it home anyway, just in case. Though, when we got there, the ice-cream tub was the LAST thing on Mum's mind.

We drove back past my school. Miss Phillips was

leaving and she waved. I gripped the door handle, biting my lip as I shuddered – because it wasn't just our class I'd told about Barcelona. Everyone in the WHOLE SCHOOL knew. Isabella in our class told me about these things called churros, which you dip in hot chocolate. Her mum teaches Spanish to the Year 6s on Monday mornings and, for the last three weeks, I'd been allowed to sit in. Mr Ashe (our football coach) told me to write down five things I'd learned from Messi. Vi and Daisy wanted me to find out if Barcelona have a girls' team and Lance had given me money for a pennant. Even Veronique was excited, though she doesn't care about football.

'Wow,' she said. 'You're going to love Salvador Dalí. And Gaudí of course.'

'They don't play for Barcelona.'

'*What?* Cymbeline . . .'

'You might be thinking of Real Madrid,' I said.

So how could I go in on Monday? The questions. The excitement. After hyping it up so much, how could I tell everyone that I hadn't gone? I hadn't just bigged up the fact that I was going to the Nou Camp, but that my dad was taking me. Now they'd know that he hadn't shown up and they'd feel sorry for me.

Facing that would be terrible and I sighed, wondering if Mum could send an email out to explain so that I wouldn't have to. I was about to ask, turning to her as she reversed into a parking space opposite our house, when I stopped.

'Is Stephan here?' I asked.

I was talking about Mum's fiancé. He comes round a lot, often with his two girls. I'd never heard of him being there when we weren't, though.

'No,' Mum said, looking over her shoulder as she straightened the car up. 'He's coming round later. And . . .'

'And?'

'Well.' Mum sighed. 'There's something we were actually going to surprise you with when you got back.'

'Is there?'

'Yes.' She sighed again. 'You know what it is, actually. I've been telling you about what we're doing this weekend for weeks. But you haven't wanted to engage with me. You keep saying you're too busy or you want to talk about it later. So I thought we'd just *do* it. But now you're *not* going away, well . . . Cym?' Mum frowned. 'Are you listening to me?'

No. The truth is I wasn't. I was looking over Mum's

shoulder at our house. I was on the pavement side and, without saying another word, I turned and pushed my door open. I went round to the front of the car, checking to make sure nothing was coming. The road was clear so I hurried over – to our door.

Which was open.

And not open like Stephan maybe WAS there. Or even as if Mum had left it open earlier, by mistake.

It was WIDE open. And wonky.

It was hanging on one hinge like a tooth that's about to fall out. The letterbox was broken and the frame was all splintered. Two windowpanes were missing, their glass in shattered pieces all over the hall floor.

CHAPTER FIVE

Jessica

Milly stared, daring me to back down – and say I didn't care. That she could have it. But there was NO WAY that was going to happen. This is something you're probably not going to believe when I tell you what I'd seen in the stream – but Milly and I are sisters. That means we're MEANT to fight over things. And we're not even *normal* sisters. You know that Milly's bigger than me, but what I haven't said is that she's actually YOUNGER than me too. She's a whole YEAR younger, which means that backing down to her feels wrong as WRONG. So there was no way in the WORLD that Milly was having that teddy.

Yep, you heard right.

All I'd found was a small, and very smelly, teddy bear. We were WAY too old to care about teddy bears – but I ran after Milly like she had my most precious object in the world. I tried to grab it, but she clung on. We carried on fighting about it all the way back along the stream. The birdwatchers weren't impressed because a big flock of ducks flew off – and Mum wasn't either. She's a Friend of Cuckmere Haven and she said we were embarrassing her. Benji was refusing to walk, though, so Mum picked him up and told Dad to sort us out. He tried to get us to chuck the teddy in a bin and, when we refused, he said we had to take turns with it.

'But I saw it first!' I complained. 'She stole it from me.'

'Rubbish. You were probably looking at a dead slug or something.'

'Milly,' Dad said, 'you're not even into teddy bears. And you've had it long enough. Hand it over.'

'Nah, I'm Gucci.'

'What?'

'Totally fire.'

'*What?*'

'It means she's fine, Dad. It's her class: they all use this supposedly cool language. It's pathetic.'

'Well, in my language, I'll make it clear. *Hand. It. Over.*'

'No point,' Milly said, running off ahead. 'We're nearly back at the car.'

Dad told her that THAT didn't change ANYTHING, so Milly scowled, stuck her tongue out (talk about dead slugs) and threw the teddy at me. One of the eyes hit me in the forehead and it HURT. I picked up a stone, but Dad grabbed my arm and, when Mum finally came up with Benji, he told her to move his car seat into the middle.

'To separate these two wildcats,' he said, though I wasn't the wildcat, something Milly demonstrated as soon as we got in.

I'd only had the teddy two minutes, but, as soon as Mum pulled away, Milly reached over Benji and snaffled it! Dad snatched it back for me, but then Mum started going on about politics – and Milly took her chance. Dad was too busy saying things like !MADNESS!, !LUNACY! and !DISASTER! to notice

Milly grabbing the teddy back again. I tried telling him, but he was banging on about what should happen to all politicians. So I took the teddy back myself, during which Milly's wrist got the *tinsiest* bit scratched. It was nothing really and actually HER fault, but Milly didn't see it that way. She punched me in the head.

Now this (as well as HURTING) provided me with a dilemma. Should I just let her win, and have the teddy? It would mean a safer head, but she'd think she was the boss FOREVER. I thought about punching her back, but she was ready for that – so I kicked her. This was in self-defence *of course*, and it really should have ended things. But Milly kicked me back – MUCH harder. Soon we were going at it so fast that you couldn't tell which legs were mine and which were Milly's, though one thing did become clear. Someone (probably her) had managed to kick Benji, which was actually Dad's fault for putting him between us. Benji didn't care whose fault it was, though. He just went off like a fire alarm until even he was drowned out.

By Mum.

Who spun round in her seat and . . .

ERUPTED!

'I'm a midwife!' she bellowed, as we pulled up outside our house. 'I work ALL hours, helping OTHER people. Your dad hasn't been feeling great. All we wanted was a NICE DAY OUT. But NO! YOU don't even care about soft toys [she meant Milly] and YOU'VE got loads of them [she meant me]! You just wanted something to fight about. Now you've hurt your brother and COMPLETELY AND UTTERLY RUINED EVERYTHING! Just like you ALWAYS DO.'

'Love . . .' my dad began, and I wanted to interrupt too. It wasn't an excuse to argue. I didn't want to argue. But I SAW THE TEDDY FIRST! But I didn't get a chance to say that because Mum stormed out of the car. Then she dragged my door open.

'Out!' she screamed.

For a second we couldn't move. Mum was being so ferocious that it glued us to our seats. Mum's normally really patient and reasonable. Even when we're not. But it was like someone had set off a box of fireworks inside her. Had we really been THAT bad? I wanted to say that we hadn't, and that she was WAY overreacting. But Mum boomed AGAIN and even louder. There was nothing for it so we climbed out, glancing at each other in amazement as Mum waited for us near the bonnet. I thought she was going to scream AGAIN – but she didn't. She turned to our front door and marched towards it with her arms going back and forth. We followed, Milly making a little dart for the teddy, though I managed to whip it away in time.

And then I swallowed. Because what would Mum DO?

Something had clearly happened to her. She normally just sighs when we squabble, and tells us to make up. We have to hug each other, though hugging Milly right then would have been REVOLTING. But would Mum ban the TV for a week, like Dad sometimes threatens, but always forgets about? Or would she make us clean out Boffo (our rabbit, who has even worse toilet habits than Benji)?

Or would she send us to our room to 'sort out our differences', which Milly would do by twisting my fingers back on to my wrists until I gave her the teddy?

No.

Mum didn't even go into the house. Instead, still fuming like some crazy thing, she stomped past the house and yanked open the door of the wheelie-bin shed. She pulled out the black bin and flipped the lid up, before turning back to us both.

I gulped. Barely able to believe what I was seeing, I jammed the teddy behind my back.

But it was too late.

Mum glared at me and shook the bin.

'*In*,' she hissed.

CHAPTER SIX

Cymbeline

'Oh no.'

I was still staring through the doorway. I was so stunned that I didn't hear Mum at first. When I did, I turned and saw that she'd followed me across the road. Her horrified gaze was staring past me – at the mess. It wasn't JUST the battered door. Or the glass on the floor. The coats had been pulled down too and the shoe stand tipped over, wellies, trainers and sandals piled up like rubble. Up ahead, in the kitchen, the drawers had been yanked out and the chairs were on their sides. It was only after noticing *them* that the truth of what I was seeing SMACKED into my brain.

We'd been burgled.

Mum's hand landed on my shoulder. She stepped

past me, staring all around as if she was in a museum, me following her into the living room.

Which was totalled.

Mum's art books and magazines had all been torn off the shelves. The sofa had been tipped over, a huge gash in the back. The sleeping bags and tent that we keep behind it had been pulled open, my eyes falling on the silver car from Monopoly, which we hadn't seen for AGES.

So that's where it had driven off to.

DVDs were spread across the floor like a dragon's scales. The TV was on its side. Mum's sewing box had been emptied and even our big beanbag had been torn open, the little white balls spilling out like snow. Mum gasped while I just gawped, in a sort of daze as my eyes skipped from outrage to outrage – until they stopped like I'd been grasped round the neck.

My Lego.

I LOVE Lego. I love the way the pieces fit together so tightly, and how the sharp corners feel in my hand. I love the two-ers and the one-ers, how you can twist them round to move parts of whatever it is you've made. I love making houses, and castles, space blasters with window pieces for the telescopic sights. Lego is expensive so Mum always keeps an eye out in charity shops and jumble sales. Sometimes we go early and queue up, so we can be first in. She won't buy kits, though. Even at jumble sales they're too much and Mum doesn't like them anyway. If I'm ever bought one, she lets me make it, but then throws the instructions away and tips the pieces in with the rest. *Be creative*, she says, which I am. I've made monsters and submarines, people and tanks and Daleks. I made a model of the Valley and one of our school, which I took in to show Miss Phillips. I made a rat called Kit-Kat, which Veronique keeps in her bedroom. Recently, though, I've been working on my greatest creation EVER (with Lance). We've been making it for MONTHS, drawing out the design first and identifying all the pieces we'd need. And it was SO nearly finished.

The Death Star!

But where was it?

My Lego lives in a big wooden box at the other end of the living room. Or it normally does. It had all been tipped out, the box upside down and a miniature junkyard littering the wooden floor. I made out some truck parts and half a lightsabre, though that didn't bother me. I could easily make them again, but I scanned the floor for the Death Star. I picked the box up and turned it over, but it wasn't there. Did the burglars steal it? I thought they must have, but no.

I was looking at it.

The Emperor's Tower was up against the skirting board. The Focus Lens was underneath the radiator. The Death Star had been smashed, totalled, blown to smithereens (as if Luke Skywalker really had shot it up with proton torpedoes). I stared at the wreckage and started to feel hot, red heat prickling up from my feet. It made me clench my fists and only then did I realise what it was.

ANGER.

And not just because of the Death Star.

Mum looks after me on her own. She works REALLY hard, but we still don't have much money. Not that she complains – AND she's really kind. She makes sure that the old couple round the corner are okay and she buys dishcloths from people who knock on the door, even though we've got MASSES under the sink.

And someone had come into OUR house.

To steal the stuff that she'd SAVED UP FOR.

I was angrier than I've ever been, and that's saying something: when Charlton got to the play-offs last season and Jacky Chapman was in on goal, he was not offside.

HE.
WAS.
NOT.

But what I'd felt then was nothing compared to this, though immediately the anger began to change – into panic.

Because what had the burglars actually STOLEN?

Mum was at the mantlepiece, scanning the photos, precious ones of our past. They all seemed to be there (phew) and I'd already seen the TV (double phew). But what about Mum's iPad? What about the Bluetooth speaker she got in Argos when the stereo broke? And what about my stuff? My Lego all seemed to be there, though I'd have to rebuild the Death Star to make sure they hadn't nicked the odd piece. But the games shelf was empty. Everything had been pulled off. Jigsaw boxes were scattered on the floor. Jumping Tiddly Frogs were EVERYWHERE, as were the animal dominoes that I loved when I was little. But my Subbuteo set was still there, *and* the Nerf gun I'd won at the school fair. Then I saw Hungry Hungry Hippos.

WHAT?!

Were the burglars COMPLETE IDIOTS?

What kind of FOOL would go to all the trouble of breaking into someone's house and NOT steal the Hungry Hungry Hippos?! (Even if the yellow one didn't work properly.) I couldn't understand it, but I wasn't complaining. I just sighed, feeling SO lucky that my three most favourite games hadn't been taken – though WAS I lucky? I hadn't been upstairs yet, had I?

What if they'd taken . . . ?

!NO!

I stopped. I couldn't even THINK it. Instead, I spun away from the shelves towards the living-room door, intending to sprint up the stairs and run straight to my bedroom. But an enormous

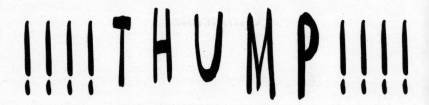

rang out through the house. Followed by another.
And they'd both come from upstairs.
'Cym!' Mum gasped.
She was staring at me, her face twisted in fear as another sound came, though not a THUMP this time.
A

Mum's eyes left my face and we both stared up at the ceiling.

CHAPTER SEVEN

Cymbeline

So . . . were they still IN here?

Were the burglars still in here . . . NOW?!

I froze – though it was more than fear that I was feeling. This was our HOME. This was where Mum and I LIVED. A place where I've always felt SAFE. I had a sudden flash of Lance and Veronique coming for a sleepover. I saw Auntie Mill and Uncle Bill arriving for Sunday lunch. I saw my parties, always at home (at least for the cake), and I saw Mum and me. On the sofa, her hand ready to go over my eyes during the scary bits in *Harry Potter*. I saw us in my bed, Mum reading to me, then falling asleep so I'd have to finish the chapter on my own. I saw us making flapjacks, Mum using a spatula to scoop the mixture into the tins, me hoping she'd leave enough behind to make the bowl worth scraping out.

It's not perfect, our house. The back window in the kitchen's a bit rotten. We stuff odd socks in the gaps in winter to stop the wind getting through. The fridge sounds like it's haunted unless you kick it and, when the washing machine spins, all the cups fall off the draining board on to the floor. The stairs creak so much that I can actually tell which one Mum's on when she comes to see if I'm asleep – but none of that *matters* because it's OUR SPACE, just Mum's and mine, and the people who'd come to invade it were there above our heads.

RIGHT NOW.

I swallowed. Mum had slipped over towards me and she took my hand. With our eyes fixed on the stairs, she led me into the hall. We were silent – until a door creaked above us and Mum gasped. It sounded really loud and so we just RAN, and do you remember what I said at the start about it being the worst of times, and those coming first? Well, as I stumbled out on to the street, I didn't think that the day could get ANY worse.

But I was wrong.

Our new neighbour, Mr Fells, had come out to see what the fuss was about. Mum ignored him, though, and pulled me across the road. On the far pavement she hunted in her bag, but the first thing she grabbed was a hairbrush. I urged her to get a move on, because if the police got there soon they could nab them. She eventually found her phone and I watched her type in her PIN, one eye on our door, which was still swinging on a single hinge.

'Police,' she stuttered. 'We've been burgled. We're *being* burgled – 19 Banning Street, SE10 9JK. Please come as quick as you can!'

Then she hung up, about to put her phone back in her bag, but I stopped her.

'You should take a picture,' I said. 'To show the police – if the burglars come out!'

Mum nodded and put in her PIN again. She got herself ready and I did too because they weren't getting away with this. I've never played American football, but I've seen it on the telly – and I braced myself. I'd run at the first burglar to come out. I'd grab a leg and cling on, though maybe I wouldn't have to – something was coming round the corner on Morpeth Street!

Was it the police?

Were they THAT quick?

I swivelled round, ready to wave, ready to point at our door. But it wasn't the police. It was just a white van, sunlight spangling the windscreen. I started to ignore it, my eyes going back to the door again.

But the van was slowing. And it was nosing towards our house!

Once again I focused on it – was this the getaway driver? Were the burglars ready to come out? Were they going to load up all our stuff, including my Subbuteo AND our Hungry Hungry Hippos?! I braced myself. I just had to focus. All I had to do was grab one of them. All I had to do was hold one for the police. Maybe it could be the getaway driver, though . . .

WEiRD.

I'd moved forward. Towards the van. I'd stared at the window, expecting to see someone in a mask behind the steering wheel, or if not a mask then a scarf or something. At the VERY least I expected the driver to snarl at me, or maybe even screech away. But, when the sun went in and the glare disappeared, he did neither.

Instead, he nodded.

And then he smiled!
And then he began to wave!
At ME.

CHAPTER EIGHT

Jessica

'*In?*'

I stared at the bin and then at Mum's face. I blinked, waiting to see it soften, like it ALWAYS does. I was hoping to see the real Mum again – but she wasn't having it. Her face grew even harder if anything.

'You've found another excuse to argue,' she said. 'So I'm getting rid of it.'

'But . . .'

'NOW,' she insisted.

And there was nothing I could do. So, VERY s-l-o-w-l-y, I pulled the teddy round, as I wondered something. Was she actually right? Was the teddy just something for us to argue about? Would it have been the same if it had been a toy truck? I didn't know, but I held the teddy out, and then lifted it higher until it was over the bin, bin-stink oozing towards me (or was that Milly?). Then something embarrassing happened. I couldn't stop them: tears welled up and then ran out of my eyes. Mum stared at me, her mouth opening as a voice sounded from behind me.

'Kath, love.'

That's all Dad said. He was lifting Benji out of the car. Mum turned to him and I expected Dad to go on, but he didn't. He just looked at Mum, his mouth closed, like he was reminding her of something, something they'd spoken about before perhaps. Something important. Mum – reluctantly – seemed to understand and she took a juddery breath. Her hands went to her hips and she stared off to the side.

'Fine,' she said.

And she banged the bin lid shut. I was relieved, but what would Mum do now? She wasn't going to forget it. I could tell that. So would she make us cut the teddy in two, like Solomon?

No.

'Wash it,' she said.

Had I heard right? '*Wash it?*'

'Yes. Then we'll see. Do it NOW. Okay?'

'Er, okay,' I said.

And I did NOT hesitate.

And neither did Milly.

I looked around, desperate to get on with it before Mum changed her mind. It was such a relief to see her sane again, though I still wondered why she'd flown off the handle. But I couldn't think about it now – Milly ran off down the side of the house. I followed, watching as she grabbed a bucket. I put the teddy in. We took turns squirting it with the hosepipe (we got soaked), though that didn't actually do much good. The teddy really was trashed.

'Kitchen,' I said.

We took the teddy indoors and Milly dropped it in the sink. I put the washing-up gloves on (massive) and then turned on the hot tap. I waited until the water was REALLY steaming, put the plug in and then squeezed the middle of the washing-up liquid bottle.

And I scrubbed.

And SCRUBBED.

And it was strange as STRANGE.

When I'd first seen the teddy, it had taken me a second to realise what it actually was. It was THAT dirty. But now, second by second, bit by bit, it started to emerge. First I scrubbed its tummy. Then I scrubbed its legs. After that, I did underneath its legs (sorry, teddy) and then I did its back, and its ears, before concentrating on its face, though I still couldn't really make it out because of all the bubbles.

'That'll do,' Milly said. 'Surely.'

'Okay,' I said. And I stopped the scrubbing and held the teddy under the tap, the bubbles shivering down it into the sink, as we just stared.

Two soggy arms were offering us a hug.

Two orange eyes twinkled out at us.

The teddy's wet fur was golden and fresh. So new-looking, almost like it was a real baby (though no way did Milly ever look as cute as that). The idea that it had been snagged in a river only a few hours before was almost impossible to believe – though the transformation wasn't quite complete.

'Get the hairdryer,' I whispered, and for ONCE in her life Milly didn't argue. She ran off and I put the teddy on the draining board. When she came back, Milly handed me the dryer and I turned it on, the teddy's ears flapping, its fur shivering this way and that while Milly did her impression of Mum's hairdresser.

'It's me bladder,' she said, sounding SO like Elaine. 'I've had too many kids. Pelvic floor like quicksand. If I jog for more than twenty minutes, I wee my knickers and have to squeeze me legs tight all the way home!'

I laughed, but not like I normally would at one of Milly's impressions. I was just so riveted by the teddy – until I turned the dryer off. The fur stopped moving. The ears stood up still, and I can tell you this. Jellycats? Rubbish. Beanie Boos? You can keep 'em. Because Milly and I were looking at the

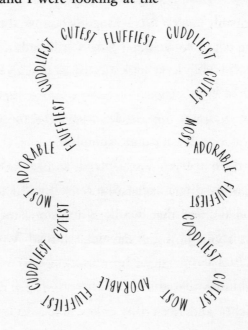

HUGGABLIST teddy bear in the WHOLE WORLD.

And, if you don't think HUGGABLIST is a word, it is now.

And it wasn't just better than other teddies.

Seen kittens playing with wool on YouTube?

Seen puppies sliding over the floor in Tesco?

Forget them. You can even forget Benji when he was little, sleeping in his cot or kicking his legs about in the bath. Because, quite simply, we had never seen anything so cute and new-looking. I wondered again what would have happened if we'd found a toy truck. We probably *would* have fought about it, but after cleaning it up we wouldn't have felt like this.

I sighed. 'We *were* pretty terrible,' I said, turning to look at Milly. 'Weren't we? And it was really nice of Mum to change her mind about the bin, wasn't it?'

I thought I was going to have to convince Milly – but she must have felt bad as well. She sighed too, and nodded, and then we both just stood there as I thought about how the day had started. Mum had been SO cheerful. She'd been working SO much. It was her first whole day off for ages. She'd made sandwiches and rice-crispy cakes. She'd sung stupid songs while she loaded up the car, then made up a story as we drove along about a naughty unicorn called Dave who couldn't resist poking the other ones up the bum. Dad had been really jolly too and I remembered again how we'd walked, and fed ducks, and played Poo(h) Sticks (EXTREME VERSION). It had been great as GREAT – until Milly and I argued.

Why had we?

It had seemed so logical at the time. All the reasons seemed clear, and right, but now I couldn't remember any of them. All I could think was that it had been SO stupid. It was like it had been two other girls, not us.

'Mum does work hard,' Milly said.

I nodded. 'Especially these days. She deserves a break. And Dad does too.'

Milly nodded back and bit her lip. Then she picked up the teddy, her fingers almost disappearing in its fur.

'You did see it first,' she said, and held it out to me, but I shook my head.

'You rescued it, though. And perhaps if you hadn't it would have been washed away.'

'So . . . ?'

'So it's *ours*. How about that?'

'Only if you mean us,' Milly insisted. 'Benji just said, "Yuck."'

'I know. So it's ours but NOT Benji's. Let's go and say sorry. Though . . .'

'What?'

'We've got to give her a name, haven't we?'

And it's odd that I'd only just thought of that. All my teddies have names. Some are understandable. My cat is called (guess what) . . . Cat. My shark is called (drumroll) . . . Sharky. But I've also got a snake called Uncle Trousers and a blob thing that Mum made when I was two called Mrs Banana Toes, which is not yellow, or banana-shaped, and doesn't have any feet (let alone toes).

So what would we call *this* teddy?

I was about to suggest something, but Milly's nose was curled up. 'You said *her*. You mean *his* name, don't you?'

I blinked. 'His?'

'Because teddies are male.'

'Are they?' I'd never thought of that. 'Why?'

'Dunno. But they are. And this one looks like a boy.'

'It doesn't! Just look at her . . .'

'At him!'

'At HER!!'
'At HIM!!!'

'Oh,' came Mum's voice. 'At it again, are we? I CANNOT believe it.'

She was standing in the doorway. I spun round, and when I saw her face I groaned. She was horrified, and shocked, but there was also something there that said she wasn't surprised. Most of all she looked angry – with herself. For letting us keep the teddy. Milly must have seen it too because she tried to laugh. I just wanted to explain to Mum that she'd simply come in at the wrong time. We WEREN'T arguing. Yes, the teddy had started us doing that, but now we'd stopped. We really had and we wanted to say sorry. But before I could speak Mum's face changed again – setting hard like it had outside.

'Hold that teddy up, please,' she said.

Milly did so, while I just stared at Mum. She looked absolutely determined, like she was planning something. I didn't know what it was, but I wanted to stop her by saying that Milly and I were friends now. Mum ignored me, though, and did something odd. She had her phone in her hand and she pointed it at the teddy.

And took a photo of it.

Now that was weird. A photo? Milly looked at me and I looked at Milly. Then I tried again to get Mum's attention, but with her jaw still set tight, she started tapping at her phone.

'What are you doing?' I said.

But Mum didn't answer. When she'd finished on her phone, she reached out and took the teddy from Milly. Then she turned away and we both watched, dumbstruck, as she marched out into the hall.

'Mum?' I said.

But again Mum didn't answer. Instead, she strode into the living room, Milly and I following. I watched as she went over to the printer and looked at her phone again. Then the printer started to make clicking sounds. It whirred. After that, it went silent, whirred again, and Mum picked up a photo from the plastic tray.

Which was doubly weird. I've told you that Dad's not been feeling that great, haven't I? What I haven't said is that he's also given up his job. I wasn't quite sure why – something about having a 'career change'

– but Mum's taken on more shifts at the hospital. We've had to cut back on things, which, when I thought about it, might have been why Milly and I were SO excited about the teddy. It was the first new thing we'd had for months. And printer ink is EXPENSIVE. Mum didn't seem to care, though – she just held the photo up to us while I frowned again.

Because the photo was of the teddy.

But we HAD the teddy.

Why did Mum need a photo of it?

AGAIN I was going to ask, but this time Mum cut me off.

'You two,' she hissed, 'have to understand that you live in a family.'

'But we do! We've just—'

'Which means that you are going to STOP ARGUING.'

'I know! We both know! We've just decided—'

'No!' Mum held a hand up. 'I'm sorry. I get this EVERY. SINGLE. TIME. You were just arguing now. Well, this might teach you.'

I frowned at the photo. 'We don't need teaching. We've learned. The teddy's not mine OR Milly's. It's OURS.'

'No, it isn't,' Mum said.

'It is! We're sharing it. We won't—'

'It isn't,' Mum insisted. 'You're forgetting someone.'

'Benji?! No, Mum. He just said yuck. And he's got millions of teddies. He—'

'Not Benji. Right then. I wasn't going to do this, but you've convinced me. I won't be long.'

'Long?'

'The post office isn't far.'

'Why are you going there?'

'To put this up.' Mum waggled the photo. 'With my details. I've also put it on Instagram.'

She turned her phone round to show us the photo on her screen.

'On—'

'And my Facebook page. And Twitter. And my Friends of Cuckmere Haven WhatsApp Group. Someone should recognise it, don't you think?'

'I don't know. But why would they? And why would you want them to?'

'So that they can find me.'

'Who can find you?'

'The person who lost it. This teddy. Because *that's* who it really belongs to. Isn't it?'

CHAPTER NINE

Thimbeline

The driver KEPT waving at me. And he KEPT smiling – and I realised: this wasn't an evil villain. It wasn't a dastardly getaway driver.

It was Mum's fiancé. *Stephan.*

And his two girls were in the seat right beside him.

I blinked. The waving now made sense, but I was still confused. Yes, Mum had *said* he was coming round – but Stephan's got a Volkswagen Golf. Why was he driving this big van?! For a second I thought that maybe he WAS the getaway driver, and Ellen and Mabel were his accomplices. That was stupid, though, and the truth came to me. Mum was right – she had been trying to tell me. I just hadn't wanted to listen. Now I swallowed as Ellen climbed out. She's the oldest, in my year, though not at my school of course. Normally, we get on, but she looked mad – at ME! Once on the pavement, she glared. I had no idea what I'd done and I stepped back, frowning, as Mabel jumped out behind her, her unicorn backpack wobbling as she stared at me.

'Thimbeline!' she screamed at the top of her squeaky voice.

Mabel is only four. I've tried a million times to get her to say my name right, but she still calls me that (something Lance has started to do too, which is SO annoying). Now I just wanted to ignore her – and keep watch on our open door. But I didn't get a chance because Mabel immediately collected herself, put her head down, and did something she's been doing to me ever since the very first day that I met her.

She CHARGED.

And talk about American football. Stephan's from New Zealand originally and Mabel was like one of the All Blacks. She smashed into me and then clung on to my leg (like I was going to cling on to the burglars). And she beamed.

'Thimbeline!' she cried. 'Daddy said you wouldn't BE here!'

'I know,' I stammered.

'He said you were going away! He said you were going to see Mr Messy.'

'What? No,' I said. 'And it's not Mr Messy!'

'Is it Mr Bump then? He's funny.'

'No. I was going to see Lionel . . . Oh, never mind. And anyway I . . .'

'Decided not to bother,' Mum said. 'Didn't you, love?'

'Yes. I didn't really . . . fancy it. But . . .'

'Yes, Thimbeline?'

'What are *you* doing here?'

'THAT's not very nice!'

'No. I mean in that van?'

Mabel giggled. 'We need it, don't we, Ellen?'

I looked at Ellen, but she just hissed and twisted her head away. Mabel giggled again so I turned to Mum. She had her eyes shut, though, and was punching the top of her head!

'What for?' I demanded, and Ellen hissed again. Stephan was still in the van, which left Mabel looking up at me, her round, freckly face splitting into a grin.

'Our stuff!'

'Your . . . ?'

'Stuff! Isn't it WONDERFUL?!'

'Isn't WHAT wonderful?'

'We're moving in!'

'You're . . . ?'

'Moving in!' Mabel yelled, releasing her grip on my leg to make little hops up and down. 'We're coming to live in YOUR house with YOU, Thimbeline!'

#worstoftimes

'Can we go in now?'

CHAPTER TEN

Jessica

We just stared.

Mum spun round, strode into the hall and grabbed her denim jacket from the end of the banister. Then she pulled the front door open.

I thought back to the wheelie bin. But this was even worse. It was bad as BAD – because we'd now seen what the teddy really looked like!

'We've got to stop her!'

'I know,' I said. 'But—'

'Dad!' Milly shouted.

And she was right. YES! Dad would save us! Again! He would! He was in the back garden with Benji. I'd heard them go out there. We had to get to him quickly, though, and I spun round, staring through the French windows. Benji was in his sandpit, digging for the little dinosaurs that we all bury when he's not looking. But where was Dad? He normally sits on the side with his trowel, digging in the wrong places on purpose – but I couldn't see him. Mum was out of the front door now so I ran across the room and pulled the French windows open. I ran out and yes! Dad was at the bottom end of the garden, near the rabbit hutch, Boffo with his black nose pressed against the wire. Dad wasn't feeding him, though. And he wasn't clearing him out. He wasn't mowing the lawn either, even though he'd got the Flymo out of the shed.

Dad was lying on the ground.

Not moving.

He was just lying there, with his arms spread out, face down in the too-long grass.

CHAPTER ELEVEN

Cymbeline

The police got there three minutes later.

Two cars jammed to a stop outside our house. Mum crossed the road to point through the door and three officers bustled in. Mum shouted for them to be careful – the burglars might still be in there. But they weren't.

'Just the wind,' a woman officer said, as she came back out. 'Your bathroom window's open. The door was banging and a vase got blown down. They're long gone,' she added.

We all crossed over after that, Stephan putting his arm round Mum's shoulders when he realised what had happened. I just stood there, numb, my head like our fruit bowl after Mum's been to Lewisham market:

overloaded. I glanced back at Stephan's van, taking in the huge, unmistakable weight of it.

Was it true?

Really?

They were moving in?

ALL of them?!

I wanted to deny it, to make the van vanish. I couldn't, and not just because you can't think away large motor vehicles. Or even small ones. Mum *had* told me. Or tried to. I'd turned my back on the subject, refusing to let the words in. I wasn't the only one who wasn't happy about it, though.

'Dad?' Ellen said, her voice sharp with hope. 'Because of this, can we go back to live in OUR house?!'

Stephan didn't like her asking that. He walked her up the street to talk to her, a little cross at first before giving her a hug. And it was my turn to glare. What did SHE need sympathy for? It wasn't HER house that was being invaded, was it? Or that had just been smashed up? I wanted to go and make that point, but Mum turned round and winced at me.

'Cym . . .' she started.

'*What?*'

Mum sighed. 'You agreed that it would have to happen some day.'

'SOME day, yes! In the FUTURE. But . . .'

'You'd never agree when that day *was*. You kept saying "not this weekend because Lance is coming over" or "not this weekend because I've got league matches". So I just thought we'd get it over with. I thought it would be *easier* for you.'

'EASIER?!'

'We were going to bake you a cake for when you got home. Mabel's been dreaming of it.'

'Well, I don't care. It's not going to happen!' I added, before doing something I knew I really shouldn't. I pushed Mum aside and ran in through our door.

I crunched over the broken glass and leapt up the stairs – to MY bedroom. I wanted to shut myself in there, maybe barricade MY door. I stopped, though, and stared, hardly able to believe my eyes.

Because what had been done in the living room wasn't half as bad as this.

My bed had been yanked out. All my books had been swept off the shelves and the cardboard castle I'd made with Mum when I'd had flu had been ripped in half. My clothes drawers had been tipped out, as had the boxes and baskets from under my bed, Scoop from *Bob the Builder* getting his first outing in years. Captain Barnacles was there too, a present from Uncle Bill, and a squishy dinosaur I'd won at the fair on Blackheath (yes, that can actually happen). I turned from it to the wall – and the empty space where my Charlton shirt should have been.

This was the one thing I'd been *terrified* of losing. My most prized possession. You see, it's not a normal shirt. It lives in a frame because it's been signed by the whole team, including Jacky Chapman who is Charlton's best-ever captain (until I'm playing). When I saw it was gone, my heart nearly stopped – but then I realised. It was on the floor, the glass all smashed and the frame broken. The shirt itself seemed okay, and that spread a bit of relief through me, though not enough to stem the horror at what had happened in there. I was about to pick it up when Mum appeared in the doorway.

'Cym,' she said, after gasping with shock. 'Can you come back out, please?'

I didn't move. 'Why? So you can move Mabel and Ellen in here?'

Mum sighed, as a policewoman appeared beside her. 'So the officers can look for evidence, love. Footmarks, fingerprints . . .'

'But why bother?'

'So they can find the culprits of course.'

'There's no point,' I said.

'Why on earth not?'

'Because these burglars just wrecked the place and they stole stuff. YOU'RE the real burglars.'

'*Cymbeline?*'

'You and Stephan. And Mabel and Ellen. Because you're going to steal my life.'

AREN'T YOU?!'

And then I did something else I REALLY knew I shouldn't. This massive pressure built up in my chest and I slammed the door in Mum's face.

Now slamming doors in our house is a MASSIVE no-no. Mum and I had a family conference last month and it was one of the things I'd promised NEVER to do. Hers were never to:

1. Show people pictures of me when I was little (with no clothes on).
2. Run out of Nutella.
3. Say the word 'Millwall'.

I thought Mum would go FRUIT SALAD (that's BANANAS *and* some). Instead, I listened from the other side of the door, just about able to hear as Mum apologised to the officer, explaining the reasons for my 'behaviour'. She talked about 'bad timing' and 'reorganising the family circumstances' – but I knew what she was REALLY doing. Her being all UNDERSTANDING was just a ploy to win me round! Well, it wasn't going to work. I folded my arms, preparing to resist when Mum opened the door again, my dressing gown still wobbling on the back of it.

Underneath were my height marks: every line that Mum has ever drawn on every one of my birthdays, each with a date underneath – in Mum's handwriting. No one else's. Always hers because it's always been HER and me. JUST her and me.

I sighed, remembering waking up last birthday, getting up and running through to Mum. Now I pictured the same thing, but with Mabel and Ellen there. And Stephan. I bit my lip, and set my face again, stepping back from the door and waiting for Mum to open it. I'd show her the marks. The history of US, all the way back to when I was one.

Would they convince her?

I'd never know because Mum didn't open the door. Instead, I could hear Stephan telling her something.

'WHAT?!' she yelled.

Mum was angry. I heard her march off across the landing. She stomped down the stairs, relief that she wasn't screaming at me turning into a question: had the police caught them – the burglars? Pushing all my thoughts aside, I pulled the door back open, about to ask the policewoman if this was true. But she was following Mum, whose head was disappearing down the stairs.

I went after her, pulling myself round the banister as she got to the bottom. When I got downstairs, she was already outside on the pavement, hands on hips and her chest heaving as she stared in horror.

'WHAT ON EARTH DO YOU THINK YOU'RE DOING?!' she thundered.

But there was no reply, or at least not one that I could hear. So I sped up – as she screamed, 'How could you possibly DO this?!'

And I wanted to know the same thing. How COULD they have broken into our house?

And smashed up my bedroom?

And taken our things?

The pure anger from before came back as I ran outside, where I immediately whacked into something big. It was a suitcase and there was another one beside it. Were they for carting our stuff off in? I wanted to ask, but instead I stopped in my tracks and just STARED.

Because it wasn't burglars who Mum was yelling at.

CHAPTER TWELVE

Cymbeline

'Hello, Dad.'

CHAPTER THIRTEEN

Jessica

'Dad? Are you okay? *Dad!*'

I was kneeling by his head. Milly had gone after Mum and, when they both came back, Mum took over. She pushed Dad on to his side and tucked his left arm under his head. I just watched, like it wasn't really happening, or it was but on TV or something and wasn't real. I do remember Mum, though. She wasn't Mum now: she was a nurse. What I also remember is that, when she first saw Dad lying there, she didn't gasp or scream. She just got on with helping him.

Like she wasn't surprised.

Mum held Dad's wrist, glancing at her watch as she checked his pulse. She did it for what seemed like AGES, though it can't have been – Benji spent the

74

whole time in his sandpit, playing. He didn't even notice there was anything different until the ambulance came. Then he just stared at us, his mouth open, a plastic spade in one hand and a stegosaurus in the other.

It was weird then. I don't mean because we were going to hospital (we were following the ambulance in our car). That's not weird because I go there A LOT. I'm small because I was born early. I get asthma and things. I can't eat a lot of normal food and have to have these special powders. Space Food is what Lucca calls them. He's my doctor. He says it makes me like an astronaut, though if that's the case then NEVER join NASA. You might get to walk on the moon, but the food would be DISGUSTING. Neil Armstrong should have said, 'This is one small step for man, but a giant PUKE for mankind.'

I see Lucca once a month. Sometimes I also go with Dad to pick Mum up because she works there too. What was weird was going to hospital BECAUSE of Dad.

Was he going to be okay?

I wanted to ask Mum, but I was scared of what her answer might be so I just stared at the side of her face. Once again, I couldn't believe that she wasn't panicking, she wasn't screaming, and, once again, I knew that it wasn't just because of her training. It wasn't just because she was a nurse. It was also – I realised – because this wasn't something that was as shocking to her as it was for me.

She'd been prepared for this.

I stared through the window, watching the city lights flick past, trying to spot the ambulance up ahead in the traffic. I tried to imagine Dad inside it, but I couldn't for some reason, as if the ambulance wouldn't let me in. I just watched the orange lines from the streetlamps sliding down the back window of the car in front, until Benji did a *RAAAA* at me with his stegosaurus, from behind. I turned round and made my hand into a T-Rex. We had a mock *RAAAA* conversation until Mum pulled up in the car park.

'Come on,' she said.

We hurried across the brightly lit car park, the bold lines of the parking bays really standing out. We didn't use our normal door, though. Instead, we went through a big revolving door that made me think, for some reason, of a really slow fairground ride. It had a sign above it: Accident and Emergency. I didn't know if Dad's fall was both. Or just the emergency part. What had happened? Had something hit him? Did he have a bad reaction to something?

I had no idea and I just stared around, trying to spot him. All I could see were strangers, though, either walking slowly or sitting on lines of turquoise seats. Some had crutches. Others had bandages on, one man with a really bloody face that he was holding in his hands. Everything was lit up by this white, flat light so that, once again, it was hard to believe that it was real. It was like they weren't actually hurt but dressing up, or making a film or something. Again I looked around for Dad, as Mum joined a queue that led up to a series of windows.

I wanted Mum to barge to the front – because she's a nurse herself. Wouldn't she be allowed? Mum waited, though – for what seemed again like ages. She gave Dad's name to a woman behind a computer, who tapped away, not seeming to realise that we were in a HURRY. Eventually she told us that Dad had been taken somewhere called 'Bay Four'.

'Are we going there?' I asked, as Mum nodded her thanks and turned away from the window.

But she didn't answer. Instead, she picked up Benji and told us to follow (though we knew to do that). I looked for signs that would tell us where Bay Four was – but I didn't see any. Soon, though, we came to a place I recognised.

'He's not in here, is he?'

I meant the children's ward, because that's where we were. Mum just shook her head and typed the code to let us in. And only when we were inside the familiar waiting area did she tell us why we'd gone there.

'You're going to wait here,' she said.

'What?'

'Carmen's behind the desk.' Mum nodded towards her. 'She knows you. I'll ask her to keep an eye out.'

'But I want to go with you,' I said. 'To see Dad!'

But Mum wouldn't let me. She said I had to stay there – with Benji and Milly. When I asked how long for, she turned away and wouldn't meet my eyes.

'I . . . don't know.'

'But what should we do?'

'Play. There's all sorts here. You know there is. Books. Toys. Just don't leave, okay? Stay in here.'

'But I'm hungry,' I said.

'Jess . . .'

'It doesn't bother me. But it means that Benji and Milly will be too.'

Mum closed her eyes for a second, then dug in her bag for some pound coins. She pointed to a vending machine.

'But how do I use it?'

'You'll work it out. Or ask someone.'

And then Mum just turned and pressed the green button, and shoved the door open.

And she left us there.

Milly and Benji were looking at me.

Play? Mum was right. We could do that. We'd spent ages in this room when Lucca wasn't quite ready for me, or we were waiting for test results. So, before he could ask any questions, I took Benji over to the little soft-play area. Milly found some toy soldiers for him, all in different poses. It looked like they'd been frozen by a witch. I felt frozen too.

By worry.

Bay Four? What *was* it? And what was happening to Dad? I was so desperate to know that even though I did play with Benji, attacking his soldiers with mine, it was like I wasn't really doing it. I was watching myself. The only time I did feel connected was when he turned his stegosaurus on its side.

'It's sick,' he said.

He got some soldiers to carry it away to hospital while I just watched him. So maybe he had been aware of what was happening to Dad after all.

Benji got bored then and started to grizzle. He asked what we were doing there, but I didn't answer. I asked if he was hungry and he nodded. I went over to the food machine, and Mum was right – I could work it. I put the money in and typed the code, opting for some flapjacks with yoghurt on. Milly said she was thirsty so I keyed in the code for some water, jumping as it thumped down hard into the tray.

Benji went back to his soldiers, but he soon got bored again. Once more, he started to whine, so Milly brought over some picture books. She started reading one to him while I watched, though I wasn't really seeing them. Because I'd realised. I saw Dad, puffing up behind us at Cuckmere Haven. I saw Mum, really upset that he'd been running. I saw how Mum had looked at him, lying on the grass. Then I saw him telling us that he wasn't going to do his job any more, which I'd always thought he really enjoyed. How he was happy that he was going to be spending more time with us 'little monsters'. And I saw myself believing him. But he was ill. That was the reason.

That was the reason for everything. I felt stupid. As stupid as STUPID: especially when I thought about Cuckmere Haven again – because we'd *encouraged* him to run. We'd got him all excited. It was our fault, and maybe that's why Mum had wigged out. I hadn't just ruined our day, I'd made Dad end up here. The knowledge was like a kick, right in the stomach, though I didn't cry. I knew that would only set Benji off, maybe even Milly. So I took some deep breaths and noticed what book Milly was reading.

The Tiger Who Came to Tea.

It was a battered copy, probably because of us. It's Benji's favourite, and mine too, actually (though it's far too young for me). I love the look on Sophie's face when the tiger comes in. I love how the tiger drinks from the teapot and how he's sort of scary and friendly at the same time. Mostly, though, I love the end: when Sophie's dad comes home.

'Please let that happen.' I whispered the words, but they still seemed to come out really loud. '*Please* let that happen *now*.'

CHAPTER FOURTEEN

Jessica

How long did we wait? It must have been a while because I took Benji to the toilet twice, and had to buy some more flapjacks. But, when I turned and saw Mum looking at me, it felt like no time had passed at all. She was in the doorway and I blinked at her tired face, expecting her to come in.

Milly was reading a different book now. Both she and Benji were engrossed in it. Mum saw them and beckoned me over to her. She sat on a chair, almost out of sight of the others. She nodded to the one beside it and I sat, watching as she glanced across at Milly and Benji – to make sure that they hadn't seen us. And then Mum studied me, so quiet and serious that for a second I couldn't quite recognise her.

'Dad's ill,' Mum said.

The words were plain and simple. And hard, like rocks. I was scared, and not just because of what she'd said. Mum was looking at me and her face was raw. It was honest, like she'd taken a mask off. A mask I'd never realised that she wore. I felt something odd inside – a closeness to her that I'd never experienced before, a different sort of closeness to the one I was used to. It was like she was opening up a new part of herself, one that us children didn't normally see. For a second it made me want to giggle, but then I went very quiet inside.

She took a breath. 'We should have told you before,' she said. 'Especially with my job. Dad didn't want to, though. Not until we knew what we were dealing with.'

'Right. So you've known about this for a while?'

'Yes. And I'm sorry. Dad's not been feeling right for quite a long time.'

'Is that why he gave up his job?'

Mum nodded. 'We should have told you. We should have been . . .'

'Honest?'

Mum nodded again, but I wasn't so sure. Wouldn't

we just have worried? I wasn't even sure that I wanted to know now. But I didn't have a choice. Mum told me what Dad had wrong with him.

'Is that . . . bad?'

Mum nodded. 'It can be. Not always, but in Dad's case . . . well, yes. Though he won't die, okay?'

I swallowed. That was good news. It was such good news. I hadn't even known that I'd been thinking about that, but now Mum had said it I realised that I had, all the way in the car and then hurrying into the hospital.

'But we'll have to look after him.'

'We can do that!'

'Properly. We'll have to change things. A lot of things. His life is going to change and ours is too. It's going to be hard.'

'I don't care. I'll do anything. Just ask.'

Mum nodded and the smallest of smiles appeared at the corners of her mouth. She reached for my hand and squeezed it – and then we looked at each other. I don't know what she saw, but I saw a Mum I'd never noticed. I saw the lines near her eyes, her left earlobe a bit red because she's always pulling it. I saw how her cheekbones looked a little rough and how the freckles that Milly had inherited had faded into her skin. I saw that she was the most beautiful person that I'd ever seen and it was like there was a bubble surrounding us, the whole world locked out.

Until it vanished.

Mum went back to being Mum again. She gave my hand another squeeze and then stood quickly. She went round to the others, first giving Milly a hug before she picked Benji up. She snuffled her nose into his neck and then, well, *lied*. She didn't do it in words, though she did say Dad was 'poorly', not ill. It was more the way she acted. When Benji asked, 'How poorly?' Mum just grimaced.

'Well, he's certainly felt better!' She was all energetic and positive. She let Benji show her his soldiers – as if that was in any way important compared to how Dad was. I frowned, like I was watching from the other side of a glass wall, one that ran right down the middle of our family. As soon as I had that thought, I realised that I'd always felt that way, only Mum and Dad were on one side, with us kids on the other. But Mum had lifted me over that wall, towards her, and

I wasn't sure I was glad. I wanted to be where Benji was, all smiles and knowing nothing, and I was still wishing that when Mum's phone pinged.

Mum had left her phone on the chair. Right now, she was putting Benji's shoes on – so she didn't hear. And she still didn't hear when the ping sounded again. I was going to tell her, but she'd see it soon enough. I decided to ignore it – though what if it was a doctor, about Dad?

So I picked the phone up, thinking Mum must have got a text.

But she hadn't.

Mum had got a WhatsApp message. Because of that I put the phone back down. The doctors wouldn't use WhatsApp. And WhatsApps aren't like texts because you don't have to answer them straight away, do you?

But then I thought about it.

A WhatsApp message?

I picked the phone up again and blinked at it. Then I typed in Mum's PIN. I pressed the green WhatsApp icon – and swallowed. There were lots of chats that Mum was a part of, all in a list down the screen.

But only one had a message in it.

'Friends of Cuckmere Haven'.

I read it quickly.

Then I looked at Mum, who was pressing the strap down on Benji's other shoe.

Then I swallowed.

And then, very quickly, I hit DELETE.

CHAPTER FIFTEEN

Cymbeline

He was wearing a check shirt. And a baseball cap. His hands were up in the air like a goalie, as he tried to get a word in. Then he turned to me.

'Cym!' Dad said. 'Mate, I am SO sorry. It's been TERRIBLE. I had this audition, it was a callback actually, and it just went ON. Could be good news, but it's meant I'm late.'

'But,' I said, running towards him and giving him a hug, 'can't we still go?'

'We've missed the flight, mate. I'm so sorry. And Alphonse, that's my friend in Spain, he's had to give the tickets away now. This weekend's a bust for me anyway. Problems with my flat, which is why . . .' Dad glanced at his two massive suitcases, then looked away when Mum glared at him. 'But trust me, yeah? We'll DEFINITELY do it soon, okay?'

I said okay, and Dad stared in through our door. 'What's been going on here then?'

Mum answered by asking Dad what the flipping heck it LOOKED like?

And then began what I can only describe as the most hideous weekend of my ENTIRE life. First Mum and Dad began to ARGUE. It wasn't about Barcelona, though. It was about Dad's flat, up in North London. The problem, it seemed, was that he didn't HAVE it any more. That meant he had nowhere to stay.

'Yes, you do!' I said. 'Doesn't he, Mum? It would just be for a few days, wouldn't it, Dad?'

That seemed perfectly reasonable to me. Do the maths! Mum was forcing THREE new people on ME so what was wrong with me suggesting ONE more to HER? Mum didn't see it like that, though. She called Dad 'irresponsible' and 'feckless' (whatever that means) and started to babble objections. Ellen, meanwhile, seemed horrified, though not quite as much as Stephan. He looked like a goalie too, but one who'd been smacked in the face by a penalty. Only Mabel seemed pleased.

'Do you like unicorns, Thimbeline's daddy?'

Dad shrugged. 'Of course. Yeah, love 'em.'

'YES!' cried Mabel, and that seemed to settle it.

Mum hissed, *'Fine,'* and Dad grabbed his cases before she changed her mind. Not that we could go in. The police had to finish first. When they had, the policewoman asked us to see what had been stolen. Sure enough, as well as the speaker, Mum's iPad was gone.

'And one of my paintings,' she said. 'I'm an artist.'

'Only one?'

'Yes, I'm fairly sure. It's all so . . .' Mum paused to look around. We were standing in the wrecked living room.

'Pointless?' the policewoman asked. 'I know. Not just burglars but vandals too. Mindless idiots. It's hard to believe, but some people actually enjoy this kind of thing. Look on the bright side, though, Mrs Igloo. The horrible idiots have made a right mess, but there's a fair few of you here to clear up, aren't there? Having a party? It's nice that we can do that sort of thing now, isn't it?'

'It's not exactly a party.'

'Oh. Well, in any case, you'll help sort the place out, won't you, kids?'

Only Mabel said she would (using unicorn power). Ellen and I just glared at each other.

We did help, though. I was up in my room, stacking books back on the shelves and stuffing my clothes back in drawers. That's when I found something I'd forgotten about before: my piggy bank. I've got twenty-two pounds and thirty-nine pence in there (plus Jacky Chapman's signature on a Fruit-tella wrapper). I was relieved to see my piggy bank – but also confused. It lives on my desk – in plain sight. The burglars MUST have seen it. Why hadn't they stolen it? I shook my head again at how stupid they were, and my eyes fell on my Charlton shirt. It's priceless – why had they left that too?

OF COURSE!!!!

I turned to the door and ran down the stairs, just able to stop the last police car before it left.

'Wait!' I shouted. 'I know who did it!'

The policewoman rolled down her window and I explained that our local rivals absolutely HATE us (and we're not too fond of them either).

'So it was . . . ?'

'Millwall fans!' I shouted.

'Right,' the policewoman said. 'I can't believe we missed that.' Then the police car pulled away.

Back inside, Dad had managed to cut his finger on the glass from my Charlton shirt's frame. Mum put a plaster on it for him, though she wasn't very gentle. She normally kisses my plasters after she puts them on, but she didn't do that. Stephan picked all the glass up, wearing these heavy gloves, wrapping the shards in newspaper.

'Well, obviously, if I'd had any gloves . . .' Dad said.

Stephan and Dad then had a disagreement about our front door. Dad said they'd need to call out a repair service.

'But we can do it,' Stephan said.

'Fix a door?' Dad didn't look convinced. 'It's all splintered. And get it back on its hinges?'

'No bother,' Stephan said.

And it wasn't. At least not for Stephan. Mum helped while he sanded and sawed and drilled. When it was done, Dad said he didn't think it was on straight, though when I pushed it back and forth it seemed all right.

'Fabulous!' Mum said, before giving Stephan a kiss.

'Yeah,' Dad said. 'You're very practical, aren't you, Stephan? Spend most of your weekends in Homebase, do you? You'll enjoy that, Janet,' he added, as he passed Mum to go into the kitchen.

And then the house was pretty much back to normal – apart from the simple and unavoidable fact that it now had

FAR TOO MANY PEOPLE IN IT!!

Okay, not going to Barcelona had been pretty disappointing, but when Mum and I were coming back from Blackheath I'd pictured us at home together, doing stuff to make up for it. Mum would have got pizzas out of the freezer and put a film on. It would have been all simple, and calm, but instead it was so BUSY. First Mum insisted that I help empty Stephan's van. Then I had to carry bags up the stairs, after which she made me put all these boxes in the shed.

'Is there anything else you require, Lord Vader?' I mumbled.

'Sorry?'

'Never mind,' I said.

I tried to escape it all by staying in the garden after shifting the boxes, but even that didn't work because

I got told off for something that I DIDN'T DO! I was practising kick-ups when Mum came out to tell me it was supper time.

'Cymbeline!' she said. 'Really!'

Mum was staring at the far wall. Our garden backs on to some garages and the far wall is part of one. Mum's been growing a fig tree to cover it up – and two of the branches were broken.

'Did your ball go on the garage roof again?' Mum demanded.

'No!'

'I've told you NOT to climb up there. It's dangerous, Cymbeline.'

'But I *didn't*.'

'And you've totally wrecked that tree. You might even have killed it! Look, Cymbeline,' Mum said, holding up her hand to cut me off when I tried to interrupt, 'I know all this is difficult, but we have rules, okay?'

She went back into the kitchen then and I just shook my head. Unbelievable! Okay, sometimes I DO sneak up the fig tree to get my ball down from the garage – but I hadn't done it THIS TIME. How dare she tell me off for something that I often did, without actually catching me? Ellen. I BET it was her – when I was upstairs. I shook my head and then blammed my ball against the shed door.

'Cymbeline!' Mum shouted from the kitchen.

Supper was some boring pasta because Stephan's a vegetarian. Ellen said she couldn't eat it because she was something called 'gluten intolerant'. Stephan said it was the first he'd heard of it, though Mum put some rice on for her – which was NOT FAIR. I'm 'vegetable intolerant' but she still makes me eat them!

After supper, I thought I could get my Subbuteo out but, with all the extra bags and boxes, there was hardly any free floor space in the WHOLE house. I gave up, intending to go back out to my football. Mum asked me to help Mabel, though, who'd left her **!Teddy of Most Extreme Importance!** at her mum's flat by mistake.

'Can you lend her one of yours?' Mum asked.

'What?' Ellen interrupted. 'Have you got teddies, Cymbeline?'

'He's got lots of them, haven't you, Cym?'

'Thanks,' I hissed. 'I'm really pleased you told her that. They're just old ones, from ages ago.'

'But you'll find a really special one for Mabel,' Mum said. 'Won't you?'

'Have you got any unicorns, Thimbeline?' Mabel asked.

I sighed and, making sure I didn't meet Ellen's eye, said I'd have a look.

I took Mabel up to my bedroom and pretended that I didn't know where my teddy basket was. I eventually managed to 'find' it, though, and I rooted through it, getting this empty, odd sort of feeling. I didn't know where it came from so I ignored it, before apologising for the lack of unicorns. Mabel chose Tiny Clanger instead. Lance had given it to me years ago. He used to love the Clangers. He did their way of talking and called his mum the Soup Dragon at teatime (which she did NOT appreciate). I'd never been that keen, to be honest, but now I could see the appeal: the Clangers live on the moon, don't they? Where there's masses of space?

So maybe I should just go and live THERE!

I didn't work out what the weird, empty feeling was until later. First I had to help Mabel make a horn out of cardboard to tie on to Tiny, who was now a Uni-Clanger. Possibly the first in history. Then Dad and Stephan had another disagreement, this time over who should do the washing-up, and who should dry and put away. Dad won by saying that washing-up gloves were bad for his eczema. Then Ellen stated, quite firmly, that there was

NO WAY IN A BILLION YEARS

that she was sharing our boxroom with Mabel.

'It's MINUSCULE!' she bellowed at Stephan. 'I've got my Level Seven coming up soon! You SAID we were going to share a BIG room! You said there'd be room to practise my arch and my walkover!'

Ellen meant her gymnastics, but I don't know where she could have got that idea from. The boxroom is the only spare room we've got. That's where they'd have to sleep – unless Mum was thinking of putting Ellen in with me! No, Dad was in my room fortunately.

'I could kip on the sofa,' he offered.

'No,' Mum told him. 'That's our living room. Stephan and I will want to be in there in the evenings. You're in with Cym, and you'll have to make do with the floor.'

'Oh,' Dad replied. 'My back's a bit . . . You don't have a spare mattress then?'

Mum folded her arms. 'Sorry.'

'Yes, we do!' I said. 'Your camping one!'

'Oh.' Mum shrugged. 'Yes, how silly of me. I completely forgot.'

I went to get it for Dad from under the stairs.

And then Mum said it was bedtime. She asked Dad if he was feeling sleepy too.

'It's only nine o'clock,' he said.

'Then what are you thinking of doing tonight?'

'Well . . .'

'Got any friends left in Greenwich? Want to go out and meet them for a drink?'

'No,' Dad said. 'And funds are a bit . . . I thought I'd just . . .'

'*What?*' Mum snapped.

'Stay here and watch TV with you and Stephan.'

And Dad went and sat down on the sofa.

Stephan looked like he'd been hit by ANOTHER penalty. Mum hissed out yet another sigh and she and I went upstairs. Stephan came too and I had to wait outside the bathroom while he took Ellen and Mabel in to clean their teeth. Then I had to wait because

Mabel wouldn't go to bed until she'd sung this stupid bedtime song: about unicorns. She'd made it up herself and it went on FOREVER. Fairy dust, candy-flavoured poo, icing-covered mountains: they were all in there. And, when she'd finally finished, she still refused to go to bed until everyone had taken turns singing the chorus. She made us all hold hands on the landing – but she still wasn't happy.

'And Thimbeline's daddy!' she insisted. 'You should go and get him, my daddy.'

Stephan had to go and ask Dad to come up. Dad joined the circle between Mum and me, smiling at us as he held our hands (Mum didn't smile back). Ellen sneered at me.

'Why don't you go first, Cymbeline? Sorry, Thimbeline.'

I tried refusing. It was SO babyish! Mabel started to cry, though, her hands making two little fists, her face screwed up and her mouth wide open. It really got me, so I sighed. And then I sang,

> *Night-night, little unicorn,*
> *Rest your tired uni-horn.*
> *Time to sleep is what Mabel said.*
> *Just try not to wet the bed.*

And we all had to do it. Dad was the loudest. He LOVED it. When it was his turn, he roared it out and even pretended to be the little unicorn, resting his tired horn on the floor while Mabel giggled.

I just wanted to go to bed. Being asleep would mean I wouldn't have to deal with all this! Maybe I'd dream of Barcelona. Or maybe I'd wake up in the morning and find out that this had all been a VERY BAD dream. So I climbed in without even asking for a story – but I didn't get to sleep. Stephan had put his phone on the landing to play this white-noise raining sound that Ellen and Mabel needed to get to sleep. It didn't help me, though. I just had to keep getting up to do another wee.

And then, after the third time, the strange, empty feeling from before came back.

Again, I couldn't figure it out until . . .

I sat bolt upright.

And I gasped.

I yanked the pillow aside – but there was nothing there.

I jumped out of bed and pulled the duvet off.

There was nothing there either, though, and I took short breaths, gripped by fear – because it isn't just Mabel who's got a !Teddy of Most Extreme Importance!

I have too, though there was no way in the world I'd ever admit that to Ellen. He's called Not Mr Fluffy. I don't really think about him much any more (I PROMISE!) – but my bed felt EMPTY. Where WAS he? I shook the duvet to make sure he wasn't in it. I emptied the teddy basket in case he'd been tidied up. Then I turned all the lights on. I searched EVERY-WHERE, panic building inside me as I lay on my stomach and peered under the bed.

But he wasn't there!

Which meant . . .

The burglars!

They were even MORE evil than I'd thought!

THEY'D STOLEN NOT MR FLUFFY!

Even now he was squashed down at the bottom of a sack with Mum's iPad, her Bluetooth speaker and her painting. Even now he was . . .

But he wasn't, was he?

A HUGE sigh of relief shivered through me. I shut my eyes for a second and then went downstairs, picking up my overnight bag from beneath the coats. Not Mr Fluffy was in there because I'd been planning to take him to Barcelona. Mum had put him in, in case I got homesick, she said. I carried him upstairs and, making sure the door was shut, I snizzled him, though I STILL couldn't sleep. It was the rain for one thing, though Stephan's phone had gone quiet. Now it was on the windows outside. Then it was because of Not Mr Fluffy. You see, he hasn't always been my **!Teddy of Most Extreme Importance!** I used to have another one that I got when I was a baby, when my parents took me to this big country house for the day. They also took my twin brother there, who Mum didn't tell me about for years because he died and it was too hard for her. Anyway, they bought me a teddy called Mr Fluffy, and he was ACE. A part of me. He was smaller than Not Mr Fluffy and cuddlier than him (sorry, Not Mr Fluffy) and I used to take him EVERYWHERE – until we all went back to the country house. Mum had become obsessed with it, because of what happened to my brother. Anyway, we went back (Veronique came too) and, that time, Mr Fluffy vanished. He disappeared, turning in circles and then floating away, right in front of my eyes. I was a bit younger then, and it was terrible.

And it was still terrible.

Because

EVERYTHING

was vanishing now, wasn't it?

CHAPTER SIXTEEN

Cymbeline

It wasn't a dream. When I woke up, I was not in the Nou Camp View Hotel. I was in my room, though for a second I did think I could hear the Barcelona crowd roaring after Messi had scored. But it was just Dad – who was on the camping mattress – snoring his head off. I blinked at him and then wondered something: how long had he known about this 'callback'? Why hadn't he warned me? It had probably come in late or something, though, and wasn't his fault. It was probably mine, for making so much out of it.

I tiptoed past Dad, and went downstairs, glad that Mum hadn't let him sleep on the sofa. I was looking forward to using it, just sitting there, watching TV.

You know, in that quiet time, in the morning, before the adults wake up and start DOING things. And getting you to DO things too. I felt a bit better, and then better again when I found the remote control: *Horrible Histories* was on. I've got really into history recently. We're doing Henry VIII. We'd begun with his dad and the Wars of the Roses, which were a series of civil wars in England between the York house and the Lancaster house. Henry VIII's dad was Lancaster (red rose) and he won, after defeating Richard III (white rose) in battle. Richard was killed and his last words were, 'A horse, a horse, my kingdom for a horse!', which I don't understand. After the battle, Henry buried him under a car park in Leicester, so, if cars were around then, why didn't Richard III call out for a Ferrari? Or a Land Rover, if it was muddy? He could have escaped then.

After the battle, Henry VII became king and was SO selfish. He hardly fought any battles at all, making the history of him really boring for everyone who had to learn about it later. Fortunately he died, though, and Henry VIII arrived! He was much better! I really liked him – until Miss Phillips told us something about him that was absolutely disgusting. She started with some *fairly* bad things, like how he stole Cardinal Wolsey's new house, and how he chopped the heads off some of his wives. These were quite shocking, as was the fact that he burned loads of people at the stake (which would have been bad, though at least you'd have had a stake to eat). But get this. In 1540, Henry VIII did something so shocking that our class could hardly believe it. So prepare yourself.

Ready?

Really ready?

He BANNED FOOTBALL!

People had just started getting into football apparently, instead of firing arrows at stupid targets all day. And he made it a crime! I was outraged and so were Daisy and Vi. Lance literally fell off his chair and Billy Lee looked like he was going to be sick. Marcus Breen had a question.

'What did they do with all the football kits, Miss? And the shin pads?'

Miss Phillips laughed. 'They didn't have those things. Football was very different back then! Can anyone tell me how?'

Marcus put his hand up again. 'They didn't have VAR,' he said.

It wasn't Henry VIII on *Horrible Histories*, though. It was the Awful Egyptians, who didn't have football because boots weren't invented then. You can see that in their pictures. Getting the ball forward would have been difficult too as they only went sideways. They did suck dead people's brains out through their noses, though, and I was looking forward to that bit.

But I didn't get that far.

The theme tune had ended and I sat up – but I couldn't concentrate. All of a sudden, this HIDEOUS noise started. It was coming from in the kitchen, but it still drowned the TV out. It sounded, in fact, a bit like someone was having their brain sucked out through their nose, only they were still alive. VERY cross, I swung my feet to the floor. I stomped through the kitchen door, though no possible explanation for the noise presented itself.

Until I saw Mabel and Ellen.

Ellen had her dad's phone in one hand and his Bluetooth speaker in the other, which was where the noise was coming from. My response was to wince – was the speaker broken? I assumed it must be, but why not, then, turn the speaker off? And Mabel didn't seem to mind the noise. In fact, she was grinning, and jumping up and down, sort of like she was trying to stamp on a load of frogs. But she wasn't doing that.

She was *dancing*.

Which meant that the sound coming out of the speaker was . . . *music*.

'The Squeaky Chicks,' Ellen explained, when she saw me standing there. 'They're your favourite, aren't they, Mabel?'

'Squeaky Chicks!' shouted Mabel, as she continued to 'Do the Frog'.

'Mabel wanted to play them to you. Great, aren't they?'

'What? *Great?!*'

'Don't like them?' Ellen grinned. 'What a shame. Mabel plays them ALL the time, don't you, Mabel?'

'SQUEAKY CHICKS!' Mabel repeated. 'SQUEAKY CHICKS! SQUEAKY CHICKS!! **SQUEAKY CHICKS!!**'

I just winced, catching sight of Mr Fells from next door through the kitchen window. He was standing in his garden, staring over the fence in horror.

It was clearly the noise that was bothering Mr Fells – and it really bothered me. I tried going back to the brain-sucking-out, but Mabel danced round the living room with the speaker in her hand. And then Stephan came through the front door with his arms laden. He wasn't still in bed, as I'd assumed. He'd been to the DIY shop round the corner. He had paint, masking tape, wood filler and putty – for the kitchen window. He proceeded to take it right out of the wall, the old odd socks falling on to the floor! He asked if I wanted to help, but I shook my head and watched, Mum coming in with her dressing gown on and yawning. She beamed at Stephan, though, while I frowned: at the odd socks. Keeping them stuffed in the window gap had always been *my job*. I'd even asked Lance for some more odd socks, when the hole had got bigger. I wouldn't be needed for sock duty any more, would I? When Stephan tossed three socks aside, I shoved one in the bin and kept the other two to give back to Lance.

I saw him an hour later. Not going to Barcelona did AT LEAST mean I could go up to Saturday morning football, which parents from our school run on Blackheath. I wanted Dad to take me, but he was still in bed. It would have been easier to wake up Richard III. I walked there on my own, the Squeaky Chicks ringing in my ears. ALL THE TIME – that's what Ellen had said. Maybe I'd go mad too and start jumping around the kitchen, trying to stamp on invisible frogs.

I was five minutes late and everyone did double takes when they saw me. So I had to explain. Our coaches said it was great to have me there anyway, and that made me feel better, and, during water break, I told Lance about the burglary. He was shocked, but he didn't know the half of it – so I took a breath, held on to his shoulders and said he should prepare himself.

And I told him about the Death Star.

Lance was stunned. He went bug-eyed and walked round in a circle with his fists clenched. When speech came back to him, he begged his mum to let him come back to my house after.

'The Death Star must be recreated!' he screamed, trying to sound like Darth Vader. He's a bit high-pitched, though, is Lance, and it came out more like the Squeaky Chicks.

Lance *was* allowed back. Dad got there ten minutes before the end and he took us home, Lance and I dumping our bags down in the hall. We ran straight into the living room, having already decided what we were going to do. The smashing of the Death Star was terrible, but we were going to rebuild it! And *this* Death Star was going to be even BIGGER than the last one. We'd use glue so it could NEVER be destroyed again (by burglars or Jedi) and we'd use hooks to hang it from the ceiling. It was going to be EPIC!

But where was all the Lego?!

I would have understood if the box had gone – Stephan or Dad could have put it somewhere. The box was there, though – right on the floor where it lived. But it was empty, not even one piece of Lego remaining. So did the burglars sneak back in and steal it?! I thought they must have, but no – Stephan had put this huge bar lock on the door, saying we were now like Fort Knox. So . . . ? Had Stephan himself taken it?

Was he mending the Death Star for me?

That would have been really nice of him, actually, and I went through to the kitchen to find out.

But I didn't see Stephan.

Instead, I saw Ellen again, and I saw Mabel.

And I saw unicorns.

Lego unicorns.

And they were EVERYWHERE. The kitchen was FILLED with them. One herd was grazing Weetabix crumbs on the table while another lot were sleeping on a tea cosy. Some were on the radio, others on dinner plates, a few really brave ones on top of the toaster. Yet more were twisting round in the air, dangling by threads from the lampshade.

'Thimbeline!' Mabel shouted. 'Look what we've made!'

She had two of the bigger unicorns in her hands and was galloping them through the air.

'Yes, look.' Ellen grinned. 'We've used up every last bit of your Lego, haven't we, Mabel?'

'To make unicorns!' Mabel cried, holding her left hand up. 'This is the queen!'

'And is that the king?'

Mabel looked at her right hand. 'No. It's the other queen. Those are the princesses.'

'Where are the princes?'

'Over there. All the boy unicorns are being banished for being naughty.'

'Then you won't need this one, will you?' snapped Lance. 'We've got to rebuild our Death Star!'

And he grabbed the nearest boy unicorn and . . . snapped its neck off.

Which caused mayhem.

Before Lance could react, Mabel did what she always did, though not in a good way: she CHARGED. Screaming that Lance was a UNICORN KILLER, she butted him in the stomach, which must have really hurt, though not as much as when his head CRACKED against the corner of the fridge. And there was blood EVERYWHERE. Not that Mabel cared. She was still calling Lance a UNICORN KILLER half an hour later when his mum came to pick him up. She was still saying it as Lance's mother put him in the back of their car, his head wrapped up in bandages like Mr Bump.

'Cym,' he said through the window, 'thanks for having me and everything. But I think I'll stay away for a bit. This place is a madhouse.'

I couldn't argue with that – not then and not for the rest of the day. I wasn't allowed in the living room because Ellen was using it to practise her gymnastics (so unfair because if I ever take a football in there I get BELLOWED at). I tried going in the kitchen, but Mabel played the Squeaky Chicks so loud I could barely hear Mum and Dad screaming at each other. They were upstairs, just a few phrases making it down to me. Mum wanted to know if Dad was going to 'at

113

least help out with the food shop' and Dad wanted to know 'where your sense of charity's suddenly vanished to?' Then Mum said something odd. She wanted to know if Dad was going to give her the money back for the Barcelona tickets. So SHE'D paid for them?! Did that mean it was HER idea? And, if so, was it so that she could move Stephan in without me complaining about it?

'I should never have told you what we were doing this weekend!' Mum screamed. 'You've done this on purpose!'

Dad said he had no idea what Mum meant, as Stephan hovered at the bottom of the stairs, trying to decide whether to go up or not. Meanwhile, Mabel knew exactly what she wanted to do: guard the pieces of MY Lego that she was calling HER unicorns.

'But WHY do you care about the boy ones?' I said, thinking I could at least make a start on the Death Star. 'They were being banished!'

'Well, they're not,' Mabel hissed. 'They've all been turned into girls. And, if you touch them, the unicorn queens will jab your stupid guts out!'

Mabel thrust the unicorn queens at me and backed me into the garden. She slammed the door and left me out there, my eyes falling on the fig tree again. Was it dead, like Mum had said? I hoped not. That would be really sad – because I still needed a way of getting my football down. Ellen had really smashed those branches, though, which was odd. We're about the same height and I've always got up and down it with no bother at all. AND she was supposed to be nimble, with all her gymnastics. So maybe she broke the branches on purpose, to get me into trouble! Wondering what else she might have planned, I looked back into the kitchen – and she was there. She must have finished her practice. She took one of the unicorn queens from Mabel, and waggled it at me.

And it went on like that ALL weekend. Ellen scrawled Friend of Unicorn Killer on my bedroom door, in babyish writing to pretend it was Mabel. And she didn't even get told off! She went on about my 'teddy-weddies'. Mabel played the Squeaky Chicks all the time, something I wouldn't have believed could get any worse. But what I hadn't realised before is that she only played ONE of their songs, OVER and OVER. AND OVER. I begged her to play a different one, just for a change, but she wouldn't, and then she broke

SEVEN of my Subbuteo men. How? By trying to play Subbuteo with them? No. She did it by feeding them to the Hungry Hungry Hippos (not the yellow one – it doesn't work). Even sleeping was terrible. Dad's snoring really was hideous. He had this really deep snore and I kept waking up, thinking that the house was falling down. But he also had another high-pitched snore that made me dive out of my bed because I'd dreamed that a train was coming. And so, by the time Monday came, something truly incredible had happened.

I, Cymbeline Igloo, truly and honestly – and I promise I'm not fibbing here, no fingers crossed – for the first time in my ENTIRE LIFE, actually WANTED . . .

to go to school!

Me? I KNOW!!!

I got dressed without any fuss. I even dragged Mum out of the house ten minutes before we normally left – all just to escape from what had once been MY OWN HOME. As it happened, though, we only just got to school on time.

There was a coach outside, and my whole class was getting on.

CHAPTER SEVENTEEN

Cymbeline

We were going to Hall Place. I'd forgotten because of Barcelona. Mum had too. She's always forgetting things: keys, her phone, where she's parked the car. Oh, not to mention the fact that she's got a son who would have appreciated it if she hadn't decided to RUIN HIS LIFE.

'Cym,' she said, as she hurried me towards the coach door, 'I'm . . .'

'Sorry?' I asked. 'Is that what you were going to say? Well, don't.'

Mum said that she'd run down to Greggs to get me a packed lunch, but Miss Phillips said she needn't bother. She sent me into school to find Mrs Stebbings, in the kitchen. Mrs Stebbings made me a sandwich and then sighed. She must have seen that I looked pretty miserable.

'It is just a game,' she said.

'What is?'

'Football. When it comes down to it.'

I didn't know what she was talking about – but then I realised. Mrs Stebbings is almost as big a Charlton fan as me! With everything else going on, I hadn't even realised that they were playing that weekend.

'Did we . . . lose?'

Mrs Stebbings leaned forward to whisper, 'Four–nil.'

'Four–nil! Who to?'

But Mrs Stebbings just shook her head and wouldn't answer, which meant only one thing.

We'd lost four–nil to Millwall.

I climbed on to the coach in a bit of a daze and sat next to Veronique. She's often got a space beside her because she tends to go on about black holes, or Shakespeare, or some other brainiac thing. She's one of my best friends, though, and I wanted to tell her about the burglary.

'Awful,' she said. 'Though non-violent crime has gone up twelve per cent since last year.'

'Has it? How do you know that?'

'I heard it on the *Today* programme.'

'What's that?'

'News and stuff. On Radio Four. It's great. You should listen to it tomorrow.'

'How can I listen to the *Today* programme tomorrow?'

'*What?*'

'Never mind. Anyway, they didn't take much. But they made a massive mess.'

'Why would they do *that*?'

'Just idiots, Mum says. The police said it too.'

'Maybe they were looking for something.'

I frowned. 'What? A million pounds in cash? A massive hoard of diamonds?'

Veronique laughed and then asked what Barcelona had been like. I just sighed and told her what had happened.

We were going to Hall Place because of Henry VIII. He wasn't taking us; it was because of our project. On the way, Miss Phillips told us to discuss what we knew about him with the person we were sitting with.

'He was right to get rid of his first wife,' I said.

Veronique was shocked. 'Why do you say that?'

'Catherine of Arrogant. Who'd want to live with someone like that?'

'Cym . . .'

'And his third wife wore glasses.'

'How do you know?'

'Jane See More? Course she did.'

Veronique did this *humph* noise and got a book out.

When the coach pulled in, we all trooped off and stared at this big, ancient house. Miss Phillips said it was Tudor, i.e. from Henry VIII's time. She took us in and we put our bags in a massive bin with our school's name on. Then we did a workshop, which was really fun. There were clues in the house and we went round in groups, finding out facts, me soon realising that I'd been born 500 years too late. If I'd have been a Tudor (well, a rich one), I would never have had to even look at a vegetable, let alone eat one. Bathtime was practically non-existent. Mum really digs her nails in when she's washing my hair, but this would have only happened once a year!

I probably would still have moaned, though.

After that, a Hall Place helper got loads of costumes out of a big wooden trunk. We all dressed up. I was only a peasant, but Darren Cross got to be a King's Guard, and Marcus Breen was Cardinal Wolsey. Lance was Henry VIII himself!

'I hereby announce that football is legal again!' he said, and we all cheered. 'Though netball is against the law.'

All the girls booed, including Daisy, who is great at it because she's so tall. She got to be Anne Boleyn and we all laughed when she grabbed her neck, backing away from Lance and pulling a face. The Hall Place helper laughed too, then asked us to settle down.

'Now then, young people, does anyone actually know why Henry had Anne Boleyn executed?'

Veronique's hand went up this time. She said it was because Henry needed a male heir and Anne was getting too old. It underlined the ruthlessness of patriarchal power. The helper said good answer, but I wasn't sure. I thought back to the night before, and Dad, and I shoved my hand up too.

'Did she snore?' I asked.

We had lunch and watched a Tudor film. Then Miss Phillips said we were lucky because there was a travelling exhibition on. It featured Tudor items, like swords and cups and books, that had been borrowed from other places. They were in glass cases, most of the class just glancing in at them and moving past, though I couldn't do that. I was with Veronique and she insisted on studying EVERY LAST THING. She got SO excited, especially when we came to what looked, to me, just like some boring wooden pegs. The sign said they were piano keys, though, which had been played by Elizabeth I when she was young.

'Her fingers actually touched them!' squealed Veronique. 'And there! The middle C is much more worn than the others. That's the same with our piano, Cymbeline!' I agreed that that was so (yawn) thrilling (*yaaaawwwwn*) to (*yaaaaaaaawwwwn*) know, and tried to pull Veronique away. Billy and Marcus Breen had snuck out into the gardens and were sharing a pack of Skittles!

Veronique frowned. 'I thought you liked history!'

'I do,' I insisted. 'I like history WHEN IT'S ON TV! I don't like it when it's like this. It's too . . .'

'What?'

'Historical.'

'Then what *should* it be?'

'About fighting!' I said. 'Or brain-sucking. Doing things with intestines, or having pointless battles with

French people. And beheadings of course. Hey, there aren't any severed heads here, are there?'

'There's one!' Veronique exclaimed.

For a second I was excited. Would I see Anne Boleyn staring at me from a glass case? Or Catherine Howard, who I felt sorry for, actually. Not only did she have to marry Henry VIII when he was old, and couldn't walk, but he cut her head off! How ungrateful is that? And, worse, no one remembers her. Google 'Henry VIII's wife' and all you get is Anne Boleyn, Anne Boleyn, Anne Boleyn. Catherine Howard must be furious. Anyway, I followed Veronique with my eyes wide open, but then groaned.

She was looking at a badge.

It was on its own, in one of the smaller glass cases. It was gold and looked like one of the brooches that Mum's granny left her, which she never wears but takes out to look at sometimes. It was small and roundish, with Elizabeth I's face and shoulders in the middle. Surrounding it were entwined green leaves, some a bit chipped. Dotted about the leaves were flowers, which made me nod. Some of them were red, and some white, from the two sides in the Wars of the Roses (Lancaster and York). The sign said '1571'.

'That's four hundred and fifty years ago! Imagine!'

'I am imagining. I like the red ones.'

'The red ones?'

'Skittles.'

'Skittles? Don't be silly! The real Elizabeth the First actually touched that, Cym. She wore it round her neck. That's amazing. Come on, you have to admit that really is incredible!'

And I did, actually. It might have helped that the badge was gold, not wood, but, after glancing at it, I did have to admit that us looking at it after so many hundreds of years was cool.

Or was it?

'No,' I said. 'It's not incredible.'

Veronique frowned at me then, but I didn't turn round to look at her – because I was more than glancing at the badge now. I moved forward, my nose touching the glass as I screwed my eyes up and squinted at it. Veronique was asking what I meant, but I just stared at the badge, not wanting to speak until I was sure.

And then I WAS sure.

'It's not amazing,' I insisted.

'What isn't?'

'This. Though it would have been.'

'*Would* have been?'

'Yes, IF Elizabeth the First HAD worn it.'

'But she DID wear it!'

'No, she didn't.' I moved away from the case and turned back to Veronique.

'Because it's a fake,' I said.

CHAPTER EIGHTEEN

Jessica

She came round on the same day Dad got out of hospital.

The lady.

Mum had picked us up from after-school club and there was Dad, sitting at the kitchen table, drinking tea. It was greater than GREAT to see him back home, but he was looking so pale. And thin. He normally shaves every day, but he hadn't in hospital and, when I kissed him, his bristles felt wrong. I didn't say anything, though. I just started telling him about the school play and how I was helping build the sets, getting really excited until Mum held her hands up. Dad didn't even argue, just saying that he needed a rest. He'd only been waiting for us little monkeys to get back so he could say hello. I poured milk for Milly and Benji while Mum helped him upstairs. When she came back, she put Benji in front of CBeebies, which she never normally does. Then she came and sat with Milly and me.

Mum told us that Dad had to be careful. He wasn't allowed to walk far and had to get lots of rest. We weren't to fuss around him. They'd put him on this medicine, which was a good thing, but until they'd worked out how much to give him he was going to feel the effects.

'He will be all right, though?' Milly was looking at Mum like the answer was an obvious yes. She nodded.

'Though you mustn't tire him out. You REALLY mustn't. And there will have to be changes.'

'What like?'

'We're going to have to put hand grips up, to help him. We'll need them in the shower and other places. He might have to start using a wheelchair for a bit and that'll mean moving the furniture about and having ramps outside.'

'Can we get a skateboard then?'

Mum would normally have laughed at that, but

she didn't seem to hear Milly. She just looked round, then said that someone from the council was coming over later.

'What for?'

'To do an assessment. Of the house. Tell us what we need. Don't worry, though, I'll . . .'

'Yes, Mum?'

'I'll be back by then.'

'Back?' Milly asked.

Mum took a breath then and looked down at the table. She took some more deep breaths, like she had something hot in her mouth and wanted it to cool down. She spread her hands out to steady herself and I noticed that her thumbnail was chipped. She loves her nails, always getting Elaine to do them when she's in there for her hair. I was surprised that she'd let it get like that.

'Yes. Back. I'm having to work more.'

I frowned. 'But you *are* working more.'

'I know. Some more again, I'm afraid. There's plenty of shifts going.'

'So . . . Are you going now? To work?'

'No.' Mum took another breath. 'I'm . . .'

'Yes?'

'Taking Benji out.'

'To the park?' Milly asked. 'Can I come?'

Mum shook her head. 'No. I'm taking him . . . to see a nursery.'

'But he's got a nursery,' I said. 'Apple Trees.'

'I know. But . . .'

'What's wrong with it?' demanded Milly. 'Mum, we all went there! It's lovely!'

'I *know*,' Mum said. 'But . . .' She hesitated. 'Because of my work, Benji's going to have to go to nursery more. Five days, not three.'

'So? He can still go to Apple Trees.'

'He can't,' Mum said. 'They don't have any extra space.'

I stared at her. 'So you're moving him?'

'No. Sandford, that's the other one. They've got two days they can give me.'

'What?' I said. 'He'll be going to *two* nurseries?'

'Yes. He'll have to. I can't . . .'

'But that'll be really weird for him!' Milly said. 'He'll have to get used to new people. It was hard enough for him at Apple Trees. You know how he was. He cried and cried. He'll be confused ALL THE TIME. He won't know where he is!'

'I know,' Mum insisted. 'I know, I *know*. I KNOW!'

And she pushed her chair back so fast it fell over. She jerked to the side and ran out to the loo, slamming the door behind her.

Milly and I just looked at each other.

When Mum came back in, her face was red. She must have washed it. Milly asked if we could go with her to the new nursery.

'Sorry. I know you'd like to see where he's going, but someone has to be here with Dad.'

'That's fine,' I said, though it felt a bit weird. Would Dad be looking after us or would we be looking after him? Again it made me feel suddenly older. Too old. I shook the question away. This was just the sort of thing we'd have to do now, wasn't it?

'We can manage. We'll do homework.'

'Or watch TV. I don't mind. Jess, get Milly some milk and biscuits if she wants some. You know where your formula is.'

'But, Mum,' Milly said, standing up from her chair, 'does this mean that Jessica's in CHARGE?'

Mum turned then. Her face went serious as she looked at Milly and said, 'Yes, she is.' She was clearly expecting Milly to complain and I was too, but Milly didn't. She looked relieved if anything, even reaching over to hold my hand.

'Gucci,' she said.

And five minutes later we both watched Mum push Benji down the road past the corner shop.

It really was odd then. Milly and I shut the door and walked back into the lounge. The house was all big and empty-seeming. I looked around, not knowing what we should do.

'We can't watch TV,' Milly said. 'What if Dad calls out? What if he needs us?'

'We could have it on low.'

'But we get bound up in it, don't we? Mum calls us for supper and we don't even hear.'

We did hear – we just pretended not to – but I knew what Milly meant. So instead of TV we got our bags from the hall and plonked them on the kitchen table. We both had maths sheets, which weren't due until next week, but we did them anyway. I filled in a quiz sheet on Henry VIII because he was our topic subject, and then asked if Milly had anything else to do.

'Only spellings,' she mumbled, though she didn't get them out of her folder. She looked miserable, and it wasn't because they were hard. You see, Dad normally does our spellings with us, on Sunday nights, and, if that sounds like a bad way to end the weekend, it's NOT. Dad makes it into this massive game. He tells us to fetch our folders, reminding us that he is not Dad any more. He's a TRULY EVIL AND PARTICULARLY FOUL wizard who's trying to make everyone in the world really BAD at spelling. He watches as we learn the words (read, cover, read, write). Then he tests us. When we get one right, he pretends it actually hurts him and, if we've got nine out of nine, he pretends to be REALLY cross. He stands up from the kitchen table and we have to stand up too – getting ready to run. He says the last word and we start to spell it out, pausing before the last letter – because if we DO get it right (ten out of ten) he chases us. We've got to get to the armchair in the lounge, which is home, because if he catches us before then he REALLY tickles us. I am SO ticklish that I sometimes pretend to get the last word wrong! He can always tell, though, and I have to leg it anyway, me leaping on to the chair and giggling, him saying, 'DRAT!' and, 'CURSES!' again because I've escaped from him.

And, though it might sound a bit lame, now that I actually say it, it's just the most brilliant thing.

But Dad wasn't going to be able to do the game today, was he? Would he ever be able to do it again?

I didn't know the answer to that. I nearly asked Milly because she'd be really positive and say, 'Yes! Of course!' But I didn't get a chance because the doorbell rang.

Milly and I looked at each other. Mum hadn't said it that day, but we KNEW not to answer the door. So we ignored it, Milly actually getting her spelling sheet out.

But the doorbell rang again.

Our doorbell is *loud*. What if Dad heard? As fast as I could, I pushed myself back from the table. I went to the kitchen window and, very carefully, lifted one of the slats on the blind. I was hoping it was just Kieran from up the road, who sometimes comes to ask if Milly wants to throw a rugby ball around in the park.

It wasn't, though.

The lady was tall, with short, curly grey hair. Her hands were stuffed in the pockets of a long, padded coat and she was wearing glasses with red frames, through which she was peering at our door.

'Well?' Milly hissed.

I turned. 'A lady,' I said, letting the blind down, hoping the lady didn't see. Then I waited, praying we'd hear footsteps going back up the drive.

But we didn't. The doorbell went AGAIN, sounding twice as loud as it had before, though I knew it couldn't have been. Milly winced. '*What if it wakes Dad up?*' she mouthed.

'I *know*. But . . .'

'What? He's ill. He needs to sleep. Mum *said*. And what if it's the person from the council?'

I hadn't thought of that. 'Aren't they coming round later?'

'What if they're early?'

'I don't care.' I turned back to the blind. 'We can't let anyone in.'

'I know. But Mum won't want to miss it. What if it is them and they leave? Why don't we just tell her to wait outside?'

'All right,' I said, also reasoning to myself that it was a woman outside, not a man, and that made it easier somehow.

So we both ran through to the hall. And, very cautiously, I pulled the door open.

'He-llo!' the woman said, in a singsong voice.

I peered through the crack I'd made and, when the woman stepped away, I opened the door a bit more.

'Are you from the council?' Milly asked from behind me.

The lady frowned. 'Should I be?'

'Well, it's just that,' I said, 'we're expecting some-one.'

The woman shrugged. And smiled again. 'Well, I'm not from the council – but I am expected. Mrs Rose?'

'Who?'

'Ah. I see your mum forgot to mention me. Is she home?'

I didn't know how to answer that. Should I admit she was out? For some reason I didn't want to. 'Dad is,' I said. 'But he's . . . busy.'

'I see.' Mrs Rose smiled. 'Well, never mind. I don't want to disturb him. And I don't need to see your mum really.'

'You don't?'

'No. You can just tell her that I called.' I was about to shut the door, but the woman held her hand out. 'And that I'm *really* grateful.'

'What . . . for?'

The woman – Mrs Rose – smiled yet again. 'Her message. On WhatsApp. Friends of Cuckmere Haven? About the bear.'

'The . . . ?'

'Bear,' the woman repeated, doing her best to keep the smile going. 'That you found? At the beach?'

'The . . . ?'

'Teddy bear. May I have it, please?'

CHAPTER NINETEEN

Cymbeline

Veronique frowned. Then she looked CROSS, which she always does when something is happening that she can't work out.

'Fake?' she said. 'What on earth are you talking about, Cymbeline?'

I ignored Veronique and thought about being in school instead: learning about the Wars of the Roses.

'They made up,' I said. 'Afterwards.'

'Who did?'

'The Lancastrians and the Yorkists. When the war was over. After Richard the Third was killed. They stopped fighting and became friends, which was VERY boring of them. Henry the Eighth's dad married—'

'Edward the Fourth's daughter. I *know*. I got

140

everything right in the test, remember? Henry the Eighth—'

'And,' I said, interrupting Veronique because if I hadn't she'd have gone on for AGES, 'they combined the roses. The red and the white ones. Miss Phillips *told* us.'

'I KNOW. To unite the country, so that one side wasn't more important than the other any more. They either used roses that were both red *and* white, or equal amounts of red and white ones. So?'

'So count them,' I said, pointing at the glass case.

Veronique stood up straight for a second, but then bent down, her index finger making little dot gestures as she did what I'd said. I watched her – but I was sure. I'd counted fourteen roses on the badge. That meant that there should have been seven of each. Seven red and seven white. But there weren't. There were EIGHT white roses but only SIX red ones! Veronique's mouth dropped open as she counted again, and then one more time.

'Yes!' she exclaimed. 'Cymbeline, you're –' she could barely make herself say the word, but eventually she forced it out – 'right!'

Really excited, I turned round, looking for Miss

Phillips. I wanted to tell her too, but she'd gone out into the garden and was taking Marcus's Skittles off him. I started towards the door – but the Hall Place helper saw me.

'Is something the matter, dear?'

'No, it's just . . .'

The helper stood up from her chair and walked over, bending down in an exaggerated way to peer at us through big glasses. For a second I thought I recognised her. As well as the glasses, she had short, curly brown hair. I was sure I'd seen her somewhere, but I couldn't think where. 'You two *are* interested in history, aren't you? I've seen you really looking at things.'

'Sort of,' I said. 'And . . .'

'Yes, dear?'

'Well, come and look,' I said. And I turned back towards Veronique. When Veronique saw the woman coming, she started to do little jumps and pointed to the badge.

'We've discovered something amazing!' she squealed.

'We?' I said. 'WE?!!'

'Have you, my dears?' the helper replied. She sounded very impressed, and more so when she saw the case Veronique was standing near. 'Ah,' she said. 'The Phoenix Medal.'

'It's not a badge then?'

'Well, it's known as the Phoenix Medal. A joy, isn't it? Priceless. Just imagine. The chain hasn't survived, but that very piece once graced the neck of the finest of English queens. Apart from our current monarch of course.'

'But it didn't!' Veronique said.

And we told her. Veronique started to point out the different number of roses, but I wasn't going to let her get away with that. I butted in and blurted it out, giving the woman room to count the roses for herself. I expected her to be shocked. Amazed even. A fake? Right here! I was waiting for her to call me a genius – but she didn't do that.

She chuckled. 'My, you are observant.'

'My mum's an artist,' I said. 'Which is maybe why I can . . .'

'But, as is so often the case, I'm afraid there's a simple explanation. The Tudors did unite both sides, and they did make peace with the Yorkists.'

'I know. Super boring. Then . . . ?'

'But,' she insisted, 'they liked to show that they

were really the top dogs. This is a subtle way of demonstrating it. More white roses than red, do you see? And . . .' She paused, noticing Miss Phillips, who'd come back in with Billy and Marcus and was forcing them to look at some old cutlery. 'Miss?' she called out. Miss Phillips turned. 'It's lovely to have such engaged children in the house, but I'm going to have to ask you to leave now.'

'Oh! I thought we had another hour.'

The helper looked down at her clipboard. 'Sorry. We've another school coming in.'

'Right.'

'Come along then, St Saviour's,' the helper said.

She spread her arms out and ushered us over to the exit.

Veronique sighed. 'Cymbeline,' she said, 'you really do get carried away sometimes.'

'Me? What about you? You nearly bit that woman's arm off. You—'

'This way, children,' Miss Phillips said.

And we walked back round the house to where the coach was parked.

I was cross – with Miss Phillips. Why hadn't she told us that the Tudors sometimes cheated with the roses? That woman had made me feel really stupid. I was cross with Veronique too for pretending it was just me who'd been excited, so I sat next to Lance on the way back. I wanted to ask him round, but he still had a bandage on his head so I thought I'd leave it a few days.

When the coach pulled away, Marcus Breen jabbed my arm. 'Why are you being such a baby?'

'*What?*'

'Well, you've brought your mummy, haven't you?'

'Not funny,' Lance said, his hand going up to his bandage.

'What was it like?' Marcus asked. 'Having your brain sucked out your nose?'

'Least I've got one,' Lance snapped. 'If they tried with you, all they'd find is Skittles wrappers.'

Miss Phillips told us to pipe down.

We did, but then Marcus snuck his phone out to do Minecraft. Darren Cross grabbed it off him and opened up a text. It was from Marcus's mum and said, Have a lovely day, my little cupcake. We all laughed because there is no one in the whole WORLD less like a 'little cupcake' than Marcus Breen. His mum needs to go to Specsavers. That didn't stop us calling him a 'little cupcake' for the rest of the journey, though, Lance the loudest because of the mummy comment – until Marcus tried to knock his head off with his schoolbag.

Miss Phillips came over and took his phone away.

We got back to school fairly quickly and, because the workshop hadn't gone on as long as we'd thought, it wasn't home time. Miss Phillips took us into class and told us to draw our favourite thing from Hall Place.

'But I don't want to see any pictures of Skittles packets,' she said.

Daisy did herself as Anne Boleyn. Veronique drew Elizabeth I's piano keys.

'Can't believe I missed those,' Miss Phillips said. 'Elizabeth played them? Well, then Henry probably did too. He loved music. Who can tell me what song he composed?'

'"Greensleeves",' said Vi Delap. 'About Anne Boleyn.'

'Yeah,' said Marcus Breen. 'He wrote it because she never carried a hankie with her.'

Billy drew Henry VIII (though he looked more like a chicken with a beard). Lance drew footballers waiting to have their heads cut off (wearing Millwall shirts). I did the gold medal. I was annoyed that it wasn't a fake, but I'd still noticed something odd about it. I drew the outline and then Elizabeth's face, adding the leaves and the roses afterwards. Miss Phillips told us to finish them at home so I slid mine into my bag, but didn't get up with the others. I just thought about the LAST home time. I pictured the playground, empty but for the things that people had forgotten. I'd SO wanted to be picked up – but now I actually felt the OPPOSITE. I didn't want to go home, though not really because of the Squeaky Chicks, or what Mabel had probably done to the rest of my Subbuteo players.

It just felt *different*.

It felt wrong, and in so many different ways.

Stephan used this shower gel that made the bathroom smell funny.

He hung his dressing gown on the back of the door and it just looked weird.

There were different toothpaste tubes on the side of the sink and too many brushes in the mug. I couldn't fit mine in.

Then there was Stephan himself.

I like him, I really do, but why did he have to keep

fixing things? Wasn't our house good enough for him? After the window, he'd filled in lots of gaps in the brickwork outside. He'd even mended the creaky step halfway up our stairs, the one I used to be able to hear at night. I'd lie there in bed, listening, smiling to myself because I knew that Mum was coming up to check on me.

Hundreds of other little changes came to mind too, all over the house, making me realise something: it didn't feel like home any more. In fact, Lance's house – which I knew REALLY well – felt more like home than mine did.

Which gave me an idea.

'Come on, Cymbeline,' Miss Phillips said. 'Can't stay here all night.'

I slouched off downstairs and saw Mum near the bike stands – with Vi's mum. They were chatting, as normal, and I shook my head. How could Mum be like that? Nothing WAS normal. Didn't she realise? Or did she actually like all the change? Even Stephan's shower gel? I couldn't believe that, but then I thought of Ellen and Mabel who, of course, were girls. My Auntie Mill's got a daughter (Juni) and Mum used to REALLY fuss over her. She made those stupid loom band things with her and did her hair in plaits and ponytails. So was THAT it? Mum just wanted some daughters? Was the clear and obvious truth that, quite simply, having *me* wasn't enough for her?

The playground was full, but I felt even more alone than I had on Friday. So I walked across it and waited until Vi's mum had turned away. Mum asked how my day had been.

'Fine,' I said. 'But can I go to Lance's tonight?'

'To play? It's a bit late notice . . .'

'No,' I said. 'For a sleepover.'

Mum stared at me for a second and looked pained. 'Not tonight, Cym.'

'Why not?'

'You know why. It's Monday.'

'So?'

'We never do sleepovers on a weekday.'

'Why don't we?'

'Because . . . Look, Cymbeline.'

Mum stopped then and gathered herself. And I waited, knowing what she was going to do. She wasn't going to get cross. Oh no! Instead, she was going to be all NICE to me again. All UN-DER-STAN-DING. She was going to say that she knew how HARD it was for me, how UNSETTLING – but that I'd get used to everything. Well, I wasn't going to listen. I didn't WANT to get used to anything. I just wanted it all to be how it was BEFORE. And I was going to tell her that, plus the fact that she was wrong about sleepovers on weekdays. My whole LIFE had turned into a sleepover, hadn't it?

A sleepover from HELL.

But I didn't get a chance because Mum's phone rang.

Mum sighed. For a second I thought she'd ignore the phone, but I could see her thinking that perhaps it might be the police about her iPad or something. She pulled her phone out of her bag and held it to her ear, her eyes opening wide. Then she turned, looking round the playground, searching for something. Or someone. Her eyes fell on Veronique, who was still waiting with Mr Mansour, our teaching assistant.

'Yes,' Mum said into the phone. 'No problem at all. But how terrible. Drop stuff round later if you like, but don't worry about it, okay?'

'What's going on?'

Mum nodded again and then hung up. 'It's Veronique,' she said.

'What is?'

'She's . . . coming home with us.'

'*What?*'

'She's going to stay the night.'

'At our house?! You said sleepovers don't HAPPEN on Mondays. And, in case you haven't noticed, we are a bit FULL.'

'I *know.* But . . .'

'WHAT?'

'Well, it sounds even worse than ours and Sylvie doesn't want Veronique to see it.'

'See what?' I said, and Mum sighed again.

'They've been burgled,' she said.

CHAPTER TWENTY

Jessica

'What?'

I stared into the lady's face. Her smile was still there, clinging on like she was a Cheshire cat (but still with a body). I swallowed and winced as Milly moved behind me, her fingernails digging into my skin.

'You want . . . ?'

The lady nodded. 'That's right. The bear. Can you fetch it, please?'

'Fetch . . . it?'

'Indeed. And don't forget to tell your mother how grateful I am. Okay?'

'Er . . . okay.'

'Well, off you go then.'

But I didn't go. I didn't move, or at least not all of

me. Before I could stop them, my eyes flicked up to our bedroom – where the teddy was. It was currently under Milly's pillow, though tomorrow it would be under mine. That's what we'd agreed when we'd come back from the hospital. We hadn't thought about the teddy there. Why would we, with Dad ill? I'd just thought of Dad, wanting to stay there all night with him. After letting us see him briefly, though, Mum took us home, Milly yawning all the way until we pulled into our drive.

'Stop!' she yelled, which made Mum slam the brakes on.

The teddy was lying on the path, lit up by our headlights. Mum must have dropped it there earlier. I jumped out, grabbed it and took it inside. Mum followed, carrying a very floppy Benji, Milly and I lining up at the bottom of the stairs.

With the teddy.

When Mum came towards us, we looked at her.

'We're sorry,' I said. But Mum frowned and I realised that she didn't know what I was talking about. 'For arguing,' I explained. 'Earlier. At Cuckmere Haven and on the way home.'

'We really are,' Milly said, reaching over to hold the teddy too. Mum sighed and took a deep breath.

'Oh my word,' she said. 'You argue, so what? Sisters do sometimes. You should have seen me and Auntie Ruth. I'm the one who should be sorry. You girls are lovely as LOVELY. I was stressed about Dad. I was much too hard on you.'

'So can we . . . ?'

We held the teddy up and Mum smiled. She looked into our faces and reached out to stroke the top of the teddy's head. Her smile deepened when her fingers went into its fur and, instead of answering, she just nodded. With reluctance, she pulled her hand back and carried Benji up to bed.

'Yes!' Milly said, and we followed them, though we turned left into our bedroom, which is when we made the pact.

'The Treaty of the Teddy,' Milly said.

Which was this.

Under no circumstances would we ever argue about the teddy again (though we could argue about other things – that was fine). The teddy would never find itself dirty or wet, or lying on its own outside. Instead, we would do everything we could to protect it, the biggest threat – of course – being Benji, who would most likely draw on it with a Sharpie, or bury it in his sandpit. To stop him, we decided to hide the teddy at all times. On Mondays, Wednesdays and Fridays it would go under Milly's pillow, and on Tuesdays, Thursdays and Saturdays it would go under mine. On Sundays it would live in the bottom drawer of our clothes chest (school uniform, which we share).

'But we still don't know what to call it,' Milly said.

And she was right. Not only did the teddy not have a name but we STILL hadn't decided what sex it was. I sat it up on my desk and wondered: DID it look like a boy? The answer was no – because who gets to say what a boy is SUPPOSED to look like? Or a girl? Boys and girls can look like anything they want to – and so can teddies. But I also decided that it WAS a boy. For one thing I wanted to be nice to Milly, but I also thought about Dad. With him being in the hospital, we needed another boy in the house.

'So all he needs now is a name,' Milly said, staring into his furry face. 'What do you think?'

'Henry?'

Milly grimaced. 'No way! There's a Henry in Green Form who eats with his mouth open. You can see EVERYTHING! I'm not cuddling him.'

'Fair enough. What about . . . ?' I nearly said Dad's name, but I stopped myself. 'Thomas?' I was thinking about Thomas Cromwell, and this time I stared at the teddy. 'Are you a Thomas?'

'No!' Milly screamed. 'Don't you remember that boy at Apple Trees?'

'The one who . . .'

'Weed himself ALL the time!'

'I forgot. Every name's got something wrong with it, though, hasn't it?'

'So what about something that he's like then?'

'Such as?'

'Dunno.' Milly frowned. 'Cuddles?'

'Too soppy! Though he IS cuddly.'

'So what about . . . Mr Cuddles?'

'Still too soppy. I like the Mr bit, though. What else is he?'

We both stared at him. 'Cute?'

'True, but we're not calling him Mr Cutey.'

'You're right. Then what about . . .'

'Yes?'

'Fluffy.'

I thought about it. 'He IS fluffy.'

'He's REALLY fluffy!'

'He's REALLY, REALLY, REALLY fluffy. He's fluffy as FLUFFY. So maybe we should call him Mr—'

'And gold,' Milly said. 'He's a really lovely gold colour. Let's call him Mr Goldy.'

And so we did, which left only one thing to decide: who'd get the honour of having him for the FIRST NIGHT.

But I didn't argue. I just said Milly should have him. I may have spotted him in the stream, but Milly had stopped him getting run over by Mum, hadn't she? In the end, we both got him, though. We cleaned our teeth and Mum came to tuck us in. After she'd gone, we lay in our separate beds, me looking up into the darkness and thinking – about Dad. In hospital on his own. He'd been hooked up to this machine. I didn't want to touch him. The machine monitored his heartbeat on this moving graph thing, and as I sat on the edge of his bed I wasn't able to stop staring at it. Hoping for the next beat. Now I listened to the house all around me, which is normally full of little sounds at that time. The dishwasher, or washing machine. The TV. Mum and Dad talking, their voices all soft as they get things out for the morning. Now there was no talking. There was nothing – until I heard a ruffling sound.

Milly's duvet sliding to the floor.

It was followed by the patter of her feet across the carpet.

Milly climbed in, like she did when she was little. I used to get cross, wanting my own space. I wasn't cross now, though. I just budged up, Milly putting the teddy between us, then pulling the duvet tight. She was silent for quite a long time, and I thought she'd gone to sleep until she said, 'He looked really ill, didn't he?'

I just sighed and shifted closer to her, the teddy between us. Which is when I finally realised. I finally knew why this teddy, of all things, meant so much to us. Dad. Him being ill. The teddy was a new thing in our life, like his illness, but it wasn't something we had to worry about, or pretend to think was better than it was, or wasn't bad at all really. It was just something soft. And warm. It was something that we didn't have to feel nervous around. It was something we could hold on to whenever we wanted, and which wouldn't change.

'Mr Goldy,' I said. 'Good name.'

'I know. Because Dad's gold too, isn't he?'

I said, 'Yes. He is.' Then I lay there, listening to Milly's breathing until she *was* asleep.

*

But now Milly was moving – behind my back. I was a bit alarmed. I thought she was going to run round in front of me and slam the door in the lady's face. I swallowed, not knowing if I really didn't want her to do that or I really did. In any case, she didn't. Instead, she turned and – before I could stop her – she fled upstairs. I sighed, thinking of her face down on her bed, crying her eyes out. I wanted to go up and cuddle her, but how could I? I couldn't just leave the lady there in the doorway, on her own. Could I? I turned to the stairs and back again, trying to decide.

But I didn't have to. Because thirty seconds later, much to my surprise, Milly came back down the stairs.

And, in her hand, was Mr Goldy!

No!

Milly had stuffed him into a Sainsbury's bag! And, before I could think of anything to say, she moved past me and held her hand out!

'Here,' she said. 'I . . . I hope that you enjoy him.'

'Thanks,' the lady replied, a bit surprised but pretending not to be. I saw that she wasn't smiling any more. 'But you found him at Cuckmere Haven?' Milly nodded. 'In the river?'

'That's right.'

'Then my grandson will be pleased.'

'Did he drop him in?'

She turned to me. 'Yes, that's right.'

'Where?'

'Where? Oh. Whi—' She stopped herself and coughed. 'You wouldn't know it. But now I have to go. Thank you *very* much.'

And, in a flash, she whisked the plastic bag out of Milly's hand.

Then we both watched her walk away, speeding up as she approached the corner shop. Just before she got there, though, she pulled the teddy out, letting the bag drift down to the pavement behind her.

CHAPTER TWENTY-ONE

Cymbeline

Mum told Mr Mansour that we were taking Veronique home. Veronique wanted to know why, so Mum explained about the burglary. Veronique didn't have to walk in on it like me, but she still reacted the same as I had. In her case, though, it wasn't Hungry Hungry Hippos she was worried about.

'My violin!' she exclaimed. 'And my chess set!'

Her mum had already confirmed that both things were still there, though. 'It's just a couple of laptops,' Mum said. 'And mess, I'm afraid. You don't want to see it. It was pretty awful at our house, wasn't it, Cym?'

'Yes,' I said. 'Awful is exactly the word to describe our house.'

Mum sighed and led us out of the playground.

Veronique was really nervous on the way back. She kept thinking of things that might have been stolen, Mum having to phone her mum to ask. I just asked them both to please hurry up. For one thing it looked like it might start raining. I also wanted to get home before Ellen and Mabel got back from their school (which was still near where they used to live). I forgot that they had an inset day, though (another reason for them to move to our house when they did). And I didn't have to wait until we got home to remember. We hadn't even turned off the main road when I heard it – quiet at first like a mosquito. Then it sounded like a swarm of them.

'What's that?' Veronique asked, as we turned into our street.

'The Squeaky Chicks,' I said, and I pulled out two of the socks that I'd forgotten to give back to Lance. 'Put these in your ears if you like.'

Veronique asked what the Squeaky Chicks were, but I didn't get a chance to answer her – because of Mr Fells. I'm not a big fan of Mr Fells, if I'm honest. Our last next-door neighbours were really nice, but he complains about everything. London, he says, is dirty and loud and full of litter (which makes me wonder why he came to live here). When my football goes over his fence, he claims it damages his chrysanthemums (whatever they are). He doesn't send it back for days, which is actually counterproductive. The more I practise, the less likely I'll be to kick the ball over, won't I? I've tried explaining this to him, but he just moans, and he gives Mum a hard time too.

About her underwear.

'Is it decent?' he asked over the fence one time when Mum was hanging the washing out. 'To display those . . . items of yours in public?'

'It's not in public,' Mum said. 'It's in my garden.'

'But I can still see them,' said Mr Fells.

Mum frowned. 'Only if you're looking. I can't help that. Or the fact that I'm a woman, Mr Fells.' She glanced up at the line of flapping bras and pants. 'Those are the things that I wear. Your sister will wear similar things, I expect.' Mr Fells's sister lives somewhere outside London, and he often tells us he's going to visit her.

'But a little modesty wouldn't hurt, would it? It is a Sunday, you know.'

Mum said she did know: because it was the only day she ever found time to hang out the washing! She told Mr Fells that she'd think about what he'd said, but she didn't stop hanging her pants and bras out – except for some frilly red ones. 'Don't want to give the poor chap a heart attack,' she muttered, as she slung them on top of a radiator.

This time, however, I was actually on Mr Fells's side. He wasn't complaining about my footballs, or about me at all. He was complaining about the noise. Mum said she'd ask the girls to turn it down.

'Yes,' Mr Fells said, stopping Mum as she went to go inside. 'I've noticed these girls. Are they living with you now?'

'They are.'

'And you have a man in the house. Their . . . father may I presume?'

Mum raised her chin. 'You may.'

'Are you married to this man now?'

'Actually,' Mum said, 'you're wrong. I don't have "a" man. I have two.'

'*Two* men?'

'Yes. I have two men here at the moment. Good day to you, Mr Fells.'

And Mum pushed the door open and we went inside, just as the rain started to smash it down.

Mum did tell the girls to turn the music down, though she didn't really need to. When Mabel saw that we had a visitor, she stopped 'dancing' immediately. She ran up to say hello, her eyes widening when she saw Veronique.

'I've met you!' Mabel squealed. 'I remember! Because you're SO pretty!'

'I'm not!' Veronique said. 'You should see Vi, or Lizzy, or Daisy. They're—'

'But you ARE pretty!' Mabel insisted. 'Isn't she, Thimbeline?'

I decided not to comment.

'Come on, Cymbeline,' Ellen said. 'Answer.'

'I.'

'Ye-es?'

'I.'

'It's all right, Veronique,' Ellen said. 'He does think you're pretty. He thinks you're REALLY pretty. I can tell. I'm right, aren't I, Cymbeline?'

I didn't answer. I just hung my coat up and marched past Ellen into the kitchen, catching sight of Stephan in the garden. Mr Fells was wagging his finger at him over the fence. I poured Veronique and me some milk. Well, Veronique got a glass. I only got a dribble because after that we'd run out. I asked Mum if she'd go and get more, but she said no because the shop up the road only sells it in plastic bottles.

'We'll have to wait for the milkman tomorrow. I'll get him to leave a few more pints.'

I sighed, then pulled the biscuit tin down from the shelf.

Now Mum has a rule about biscuits. After school, I have to have one PLAIN biscuit first, such as a digestive, ginger nut or custard cream. It's a bit like having to eat your vegetables. After that, I am allowed ONE regular-sized CHOCOLATE biscuit or TWO chocolate fingers. It's a tricky choice to make, though today I was hoping Mum would let me break the rule because of Veronique's burglary. But she couldn't. Yesterday there'd been a WHOLE PILE of Jaffa Cakes in the tin, the top of each one as shiny as a fresh conker. But when I opened the lid that afternoon it was like a demolition site: just crumbs, lumps and a couple of broken triangles.

'Sorry, Cymbeline,' Ellen said, with a big, fake smile.

'Great,' I said.

Veronique said she didn't mind. Ellen went into the living room while I tipped the crumbs out on to plates.

We sat at the kitchen table and Veronique went serious.
'It's so weird,' she said, 'to think of people breaking
into your house.'

'I know. Especially as they burgled us too.'

'They?' Veronique licked the end of her finger and
used it pick up biscuit crumbs. 'You don't mean "they"
like it was the same lot of burglars, do you?'

I shrugged. 'My house. Your house. It is a bit of a
coincidence.'

'Really? I mean, it would be if we lived closer to
each other. There might be a gang in the area, going
round local houses. But I live miles away.'

I turned round. 'Mum?' I said. 'How did the
burglars get into Veronique's house?'

'Broke the door down, I'm afraid. Oh.' Mum's face
lit up. 'I wonder if Stephan could go round and . . .'
She hurried through to the garden.

'See?' I said, but Veronique wasn't impressed.

'It's not like it's an uncommon way of getting in.'

'True, but it doesn't look like they stole much at
yours, just like here. They even left my piggy bank.'

'Maybe they didn't want to steal from a kid.'

'After they'd trashed my room? They didn't care
about *that*, did they?'

'No, I suppose not. Well, maybe it was the same people. But it's still not that unusual. Non-violent crime has gone up twelve per cent since last year. Did you listen to the *Today* programme this morning?'

I had, actually. And I still couldn't quite get it, because everything they were talking about seemed to have happened *yesterday*. I also thought it odd that Veronique didn't remember what she herself had said about our burglary: that the burglars might have gone into our house for a specific reason.

'So maybe they *were* looking for something,' I said. 'They didn't find it at our house so they broke into yours?'

'But what?' Veronique said, tipping the last of the crumbs into her cupped hand.

I shrugged. I had absolutely no idea.

'Right,' Mum said, coming back inside with Stephan, who had his toolbox in his hand. 'Homework.'

She meant all of us. Mabel didn't have any of course as she's only in Reception, but she joined us at the table anyway (to draw unicorns). Ellen and Veronique both got maths sheets out and I could tell that, secretly, Ellen was impressed: Miss Phillips gives Veronique super-hard things to do, her sheet littered with all these funny boxes, brackets and squiggles (like hieroglyphs off *Awful Egyptians*). That actually shut Ellen up for a second or two, until she turned to me.

'Well, Cymbeline? Aren't you going to get *your* maths out?'

The answer was no – not in front of her. Maths isn't my greatest subject in the world. Instead, I pulled out my picture of Elizabeth I's medal. I sat up straight and spread it out in front of me so Ellen could get a proper eyeful – because I'm good at art. It's the one school subject I am good at, because of Mum. Ever since I was little, I've been going with her when she runs art workshops at galleries and playgroups, picking up tips along the way.

I wanted some now because I was stuck. I was proud of what I'd done so far – especially the ruffles round Elizabeth I's neck – but my picture didn't quite look real. I couldn't work out why until I remembered: though Elizabeth was looking to the right on the medal, like a pharaoh on the side of a sarcophagus, the medal wasn't quite flat. It was made out of metal so there were little shadows on it – which I hadn't done. As soon as I realised that, I wanted to add them, but I hesitated. The picture had taken me quite a long time and I wasn't sure about shadows. I didn't want to ruin it.

I turned round, wanting Mum to show me, but she was out on the pavement, giving Stephan directions to Veronique's house. He drove off and I thought she'd come in, but Dad showed up then and Mum and he started to have a 'conversation'. Mum asked Dad if he'd sorted out a new place to live, and Dad wanted to know if she was enjoying living with Bob the Builder. I think he meant Stephan. I sighed and turned back, thinking I could have a little go at the shadowing, but Ellen was now looking at my picture.

'What's that?'

I told her – about Hall Place. 'It was amazing,' I said. 'We saw some piano keys that had actually been played by Elizabeth the First.' Veronique glanced up from her maths, giving me a funny look. 'And this is a medal she actually wore.'

'Well, it's wrong,' Ellen said.

'You can do better? Show me then. Draw something.'

'I didn't mean that.' Ellen pointed at my picture. 'We're doing the Tudors too. There was Lancaster and York and then it was all joined. You've got the wrong number of roses.'

'Oh,' I said. 'Have I?'

And (without mentioning that I'd thought that too) I told her how the Tudors liked to show they were top dogs. Ellen said I was making it up, but Veronique glanced away from her maths again.

'It's true,' she said. And I thought that would shut Ellen UP.

But it didn't.

At first Ellen seemed annoyed. But then she sat up, a thought coming to her that made her smile. 'Wow, Veronique, that maths looks hard.'

Veronique bit the top of her pencil. 'Not really. It's just about understanding which fractional component is . . .'

'Can you show me?' Ellen said.

Showing Ellen meant Veronique switching places with me. She did sums on some scrap paper while Ellen watched, asking questions and telling Veronique how brilliant she was.

'You should be a teacher!' she said. 'I can so understand, the way you say it.'

'Thanks,' Veronique replied. 'Though after my PhD I'll be going into research. I'll—'

'Do you like reading?' Ellen asked.

Veronique said she did. Ellen asked what she was reading, then got Veronique to tell her all about *A Tale of Two Cities*. Ellen said it sounded amazing.

'Have you read any more Charles Dickens?'

'Oh yes,' Veronique said. '*Great Expectations* is brilliant.'

'Can I borrow it?'

'Borrow . . . ? Of course. It would be great to have someone to discuss it with. It's the same with music. No one really—'

'But I love music!' Ellen said, and she reached for her dad's phone, which he'd forgotten. She turned the speaker on, and I thought she was going to blitz us with the Squeaky Chicks, making Veronique wince. But piano music started to play.

'Rachmaninoff!' Veronique exclaimed. 'My favourite!'

'Really? Mine too! Do you play?'

'Yes. I'd show you but they haven't got a piano here.'

'I KNOW!' Ellen sighed. 'So annoying. I've brought my ukulele, though. Want to come upstairs and play that with me?'

'Great,' Veronique said.

And, without glancing at me, Veronique and Ellen pushed their chairs back and ran upstairs.

I was angry. I'd thought that, after our homework, I could take Veronique to my room and make some space for my Subbuteo. She's getting better every single time we play. I sighed, and prepared myself to wait until Veronique had finished playing the ukulele with Ellen. But they played it for AGES, after which Veronique taught Ellen how to do the Rubik's cube that she'd given me for Christmas (still in its box).

After *that*, Ellen showed Veronique her walkovers and handstands, and THEN they did each other's hair! I didn't even know Veronique cared about hair. She normally only has a ponytail, but Ellen did all sorts of things to it while they both COMPLETELY ignored me. I should have joined in, and I sort of wanted to, because footballers are really into doing their hair too. Lance says that the managers make them, because of the TV cameras. My hair's only a centimetre long, though, and Ellen and Veronique continued to ignore me anyway, Ellen pulling Veronique over to sit next to HER at the dinner table. They chatted away to each other as if they were in a soundproof box and couldn't hear anything

I said. I gave up trying to get them to listen and turned to Dad, who was leaning towards Mum and telling her all about his latest casting. He was doing all the other actors' voices and Mum was actually laughing, in spite of herself. Mabel laughed too.

'Tell that to my daddy,' she said. 'When he gets back from mending the door!'

'Sure,' said Dad. 'No problem.'

He turned back to Mum, but for some reason she didn't want to listen any more, just concentrating on her dinner.

And then we'd finished.

Ellen asked if she could take Veronique off to watch TV. Mum said yes and so, of course, I pushed my chair back too. I was about to suggest *Horrible Histories*, but Dad put his hand on my arm.

'Why not help me with the washing-up?' he said. 'Dad and son bonding over bubbles, yeah? Got to make ourselves useful around here, don't you think?'

'But they're not doing anything!' I said, pointing at the two girls as they laughed their way out of the door.

'Veronique's our guest,' Mum said. 'Why not let her and Ellen enjoy themselves? Ellen can help tomorrow, can't she?'

I sighed, and shook my head, and did the washing-up as fast as I could. Then I went through to the living room and sat on the edge of the sofa. But Veronique and Ellen didn't even notice me, just gawping bug-eyed at the screen. And not at *Horrible Histories*. Ellen had put on this programme set at a gymnastics club. Boys and girls in shiny leotards were doing flick flacks on a big mat, which looked pointless to me. Without a ball, and goals, it was so, well, empty.

'What's going on?' I said.

But they were both so riveted that neither of them answered me. I asked again and got the same result – so I gave up. I went to play Subbuteo, on my own (which had to be five-a-side because half my players were recovering from hippo-related injuries).

It would be better at bedtime, though – I was sure. I already knew that Dad would be sleeping on the sofa. I was looking forward to being with Veronique in my room – so that we could talk about the burglaries. Maybe we could work out what the burglars might have been searching for. But, once I'd finished cleaning my teeth, I came out and saw Mum in there: and she wasn't just sorting out Veronique.

Ellen was in there too.

'You don't mind do you, Cym?' she asked, though I didn't know what she meant. I presumed that Ellen was just coming in to say goodnight or something. Veronique was already in a sleeping bag, on the camping mattress. But then I watched as, almost in slow motion, Ellen did something that I couldn't quite believe I was seeing.

She climbed into MY bed!

'MIND!!!' I said. 'Of course I mind! What do you think . . .'

'Come on, Cym,' Mum said. 'It's probably more appropriate this way.'

'Appropriate? What does that mean?'

'Well, being girls.'

'Girls? You're always telling me there's no difference. And it's true. Vi and Daisy, for instance. They play football even more than me! And they foul! Vi nearly kicked my leg off on Saturday, and Daisy elbowed me in the head. Twice. Anyway, you say I should be friends with boys and girls.'

'I know. But . . .' Mum paused, and ushered me out. On the landing she whispered, 'Ellen and Veronique are getting on really well.'

'I've noticed that.'

'Ellen doesn't have any friends around here yet, does she?'

'So?'

'She needs some. To make her feel at home, don't you think?'

'Not if they're MY friends! Tell her to get her own.'

'How, Cym?'

'Don't ask me. She can put a notice in the window or something. "New Girl Requires Friends Who Won't Mind That She's Horrible". I don't care. And she's in MY BED. You are SO going to have to buy me a new one tomorrow.'

'A new bed? Why?'

'Well, I'm not sleeping in that one again NOW, am I? EEUURRGH! And aren't you forgetting something? Now that you've kicked me out of MY bed, and MY bedroom, where am I supposed to sleep? On the sofa?'

'Your dad'll be on that.'

'Then . . . ?'

'You can sleep with ME, Thimbeline!'

Mabel. I was surprised that she'd said it, actually, seeing as I was the Friend of a Unicorn Killer, and everything.

'It's okay,' she said, after Mum had practically

177

shoved me into the boxroom. 'I like you again now because you've given Veronique to us. But go on.'

'Go on what?'

'You know, silly!'

And so I had to do it – sing Mabel's 'Night-Night, Unicorn' song. She didn't want anyone else joining in, but did want the same amount of goes through. So I had to sing it six times, Mabel making me start again if I either mumbled, or wasn't loud enough. It was so embarrassing, especially when I heard giggling coming out of my bedroom.

'Lovely,' Mum said. 'But hop into bed now, you two.'

So we did, Mabel on one blow-up mattress and me on the other. She fell asleep straight away, but I couldn't. For a start it was like she was Dad's daughter, not Stephan's – she SNORED TOO! It was like lying next to an episode of *Peppa Pig*. Also, I'd left Not Mr Fluffy in my room and couldn't bring myself to go in there to get him, not after Ellen's 'teddy-weddies' comment. Then there was the raining sound. I kept needing to wee again and, when I came back after the THIRD time, Mabel had half rolled out of her bed and was lying over mine. I hissed, and went downstairs to get

Mum to move her (Stephan was still out). Mum was in the living room. I could hear her through the closed door, with Dad. Oddly, they weren't arguing, though.

'Definitely 2009,' Dad said. 'That was the best year. Springsteen was unbelievable!'

'Not as good as Blur!'

'You kidding? The Boss every time. And neither was as good as the sight of you sitting in that puddle when you fell off my shoulders!'

'Fell off?' Mum screeched. 'You dumped me. You SO dumped me!'

I had no idea what they were on about, but it was great that they weren't trying to kill each other. I decided not to bother them and went through to the kitchen for a glass of milk – only remembering that we didn't have any when the light in the fridge came on. It lit up the kitchen and all of our homework on the worktop. I saw my picture and I remembered that I still hadn't found out how to do shadowing. I wanted to show it to Miss Phillips in the morning and I turned towards the living room – but Mum was still laughing.

'And we got in that tent and fell asleep . . .'

'But it wasn't our tent!' Dad roared.

No. They were still talking gibberish, but I'd leave

them to it. Mum's mobile was on the side, though, sitting on Veronique's maths sheet.

Would there be a picture somewhere? One I could copy?

I tapped in Mum's PIN and went on the Internet.

Google search: Elizabeth I's medal.

Nothing.

My mind went back to Hall Place and the helper. 'The Phoenix Medal'. That's what she'd called it.

I typed that in and up it came, the medal I'd seen that very day, and which I was making a copy of. It was part of something called 'The British Museum Permanent Collection', though it was currently out on loan – which is why I'd seen it. I clicked on the image and it filled the screen, the little bits of shading clearly visible. Glad that I was right about that, I turned the kitchen light on and sat down, adding a little bit of shadow to my picture and then glancing at the phone, the picture really coming to life in front of me.

Until I stopped glancing.

I'd been about to turn the phone off. I'd finished my drawing and I was really pleased with it, but tired. I didn't care that Mum and Dad were laughing. I'd get Mum to move Mabel and then I'd go to sleep.

But the roses.

The RED roses and the WHITE roses.

In the picture on Mum's phone, there were fourteen of them – like in my copy. I counted twice to make sure.

Yes, fourteen roses.

At Hall Place there had been EIGHT white ones and SIX red ones.

But HERE there were seven red roses.

And seven white ones.

There were EXACTLY THE SAME number of each.

What could it mean?

CHAPTER TWENTY-TWO

Jessica

Mum and Benji came back half an hour after the woman had left. Five minutes after that, the man from the council actually arrived. He and Mum went from room to room, making notes, Mum's face falling further with every passing minute.

'That much?' I heard her say at one point. When he'd gone, I asked about the nursery.

'Is it nice?'

'It's fine,' Mum said.

'So is Benji going there?'

'I don't know. The fees are higher than Apple Trees. After my travel, and my tax . . . I don't know. Anyway, what did you two get up to?'

I was about to shrug and just say homework, but

Milly came in from the lounge – and she told her. She described the lady and how we'd been careful not to let her in. Mum winced.

'But you gave her the teddy?' Milly nodded. 'I'm sorry, girls. I shouldn't have done it. You found something that cheered you up and got you excited. Something that was just . . . nice. I overreacted, though some little boy is going to be pleased at least. Mrs . . . ?'

'Rose.'

'That's right. Well, I'll make it up to you, I promise.'

I said not to bother and turned to Milly, not quite able to believe the way she was acting. I was PRETENDING not to mind about Mr Goldy because I didn't want Mum to worry about one more thing. But Milly looked like she actually didn't CARE. She was either a much better actor than me, or the teddy didn't mean anything near as much to her as she'd said. I was cross with her and I wanted to tell her off, but that wouldn't bring Mr Goldy back, would it?

One thing did bother me, though.

'Mum,' I said. 'How did Mrs Rose find you?'

'Oh. I got a text. She said she'd tried to contact

me on WhatsApp the other day, but I didn't get that. She said her son dropped his teddy in the river.'

'Oh. She told us it was her grandson.'

'What?'

'She said her grandson dropped it.'

'Then I must have got that wrong. Or maybe she's the main carer. What does it matter? Someone will be really happy, though I'm still very sorry. That bear, it really was cute, wasn't it?'

'Yes.'

'And soft after you'd washed it. It was really . . .' Mum was searching for the word.

'Fluffy?'

'That's right! Fluffy. It was really, really fluffy. But I suppose you'll just have to move on, okay?'

I said okay, but then thought about Mr Goldy and how he'd felt, between Milly and me, after she'd climbed in my bed. And I thought about Mum talking to me at the hospital, and how it had made me feel much older than I was.

I wanted Milly to get in that night, and I asked her. But she said, 'No, I'm Gucci.'

I laughed. 'Can't you learn some more "cool" words?' I said. 'I'm bored of that one.'

Milly just went ha ha, and I expected her to stick her tongue out at me. She didn't, though. She was completely covered by her duvet and she stayed that way. I listened to her scruffling about before she went to sleep.

In the morning, I could tell that something was different. When I walked downstairs, I saw what it was. The house was bright and busy, like I was late for something. Mum had obviously been up for hours. Cupboards were open and drawers pulled out. There were piles of toys, clothes and books everywhere.

'I'm having a clear-out,' Mum explained from the top of a stepladder.

'Now?'

I pulled my slippers on, then picked up some pairs of really diddy socks from the nearest pile. It was hard to believe that they'd fitted all of us once. I put them down and looked at a little board book that even Benji was too old for. It had lived on the side of his buggy and was a bit battered. Then I picked up what looked like a small cooking pot, long, thin forks Sellotaped to the side.

'What's this?'

Mum turned her head. 'A fondue set.'

'What's fondue?'

'Something we never make, which is why I'm getting rid of the fondue set.'

I put *that* down and picked up a green corduroy dress that had been both Milly's *and* mine. It was too small now but still pretty, and it seemed like a waste to be getting rid of it.

'Benji wouldn't care,' I said, holding it up. 'Perhaps you could stitch some dinosaurs on the front.'

Mum laughed. 'I don't think so.'

I put the dress back – and then frowned. There was something sad about all this stuff leaving our house, even if we didn't need it any more. 'Where are you taking it all? Oxfam?'

Mum made her way down the ladder. 'No. I thought we'd try to sell it. There's a car-boot sale at the station on Sunday. Can you dig some things out? There's loads of stuff you don't play with any more.'

My first instinct was to say no, but I knew that there actually were things I didn't want. I said I'd do it after school.

Milly came down then, and we had breakfast. Back upstairs I saw, to my surprise, that she'd got my school uniform out for me. It was really nice of her. I put it on and by the time we were both ready we had a surprise: Dad was downstairs. And he was dressed. He was insisting on taking us to school, though Mum wasn't sure. Brighton (where we live) is really hilly and our house is at the top of one. Our school is at the bottom and Dad couldn't possibly walk back up. Not the way he was feeling. But he said he'd drive us.

'I know I shouldn't, but maybe just for a week or two. Till I'm feeling better. I'll drop you at the hospital after, love, okay?'

Mum hesitated but nodded. Once she'd walked Benji round to Apple Trees, the four of us got in the car. And I was pleased – to begin with. Dad drove and for a minute or two it was just like it always had been (though we never drive to school). But, when we got there, it was strange. I thought Dad would drop us off, Mum maybe taking us in or just kissing us goodbye in the car. It wasn't like we didn't know where to go. But Dad insisted on parking – so that he could come into the playground with the other parents. And I swallowed. He's always been amazing, Dad has. He's tall and fit. Until recently, he still played

187

loads of football, as well as watching his beloved Seagulls (the Brighton team). He used to do park runs on Saturday mornings and once did a half-marathon along the seafront. We made a big banner for him! At the school fair he's always in charge of putting the outdoor stage together, not needing any help to lift the huge pieces into place. It doesn't matter what size you are of course (I should know that!), but I've always loved the fact that he's big and strong. It makes up for me somehow.

But now he was anything *but* strong.

When Dad got out of the car, it was a real struggle for him. He had to take a few breaths, leaning against the open door. Then he hobbled up the street towards the gates, his face pale, some sweat on his brow, Mum holding on to his arm.

'Dad,' I said. 'You don't have to. You can say goodbye here. It's fine.'

'No!' he said. 'I can do it, love.'

I just stood there, wincing with every movement he made, feeling TOTALLY and UTTERLY ashamed of myself.

You see, I hadn't told Dad to leave us there to be nice to him. Or to make sure he was okay. I'd said it because I didn't want him to come. Kids were already looking at him. Two mums stopped to let him past, one pulling the sleeve of the other one's coat and whispering. When we got into the playground, even more kids started looking at him. A football flew towards him and he made this USELESS attempt to pass it back. It was worse than I would have done. He made a joke about being so bad he could get in the Brighton team, but the kid just looked a bit scared. He took the ball and ran away. Then, when Dad held his hands out to me, to say goodbye, I winced: because they were shaking. I didn't want to go to him. I didn't want to kiss him goodbye. That made me feel worse than I'd ever felt in my whole life.

And it was a feeling that lasted all day.

What was I like? What sort of person was inside me, making me feel these things? My dad was my dad and I loved him, so why was I . . . ashamed of him? All morning I was quiet and at lunchtime I sat in the playground on my own, thinking about this secret self inside me that was really and truly horrible. Then I had a worse thought – what if Dad had been able to tell? What if he'd guessed that I was feeling the way I was? About him? I took a long, cold breath, the thought almost too much to bear. I'd make it up to him. Whatever I felt, I'd hide it, not just from him but everyone. Who would ever want to be my friend if they knew what I was thinking about my OWN dad?

'You all right, Jess?'

It was Mr Michaels, our music teacher. He was on playground duty. I just nodded, once again horrified that I could feel the things that I was feeling. Then I ran inside.

The secret sat inside my stomach for the rest of the day like a lump of wet clay. It was still there at home time. I'm allowed to walk Milly home after school, but I had a sudden fear: that Dad would come to meet us. When he wasn't there, I was relieved, but that relief seemed to twist and turn inside me when I realised how bad it was of me to feel it. But I did feel it and, when I looked round at all the other parents, picking up all the other kids, I couldn't help wishing that Dad was like them: normal. With nothing wrong with him.

'What's the matter?'

I turned to Milly and stared at her in horror – because what if SHE knew how I was feeling? I said,

'Nothing,' and told her that we'd better get a move on.

Which we did, though we didn't go straight home.

We walked up Elm Road and turned right past the church. A girl from Milly's class lives there and we waved at her as she opened her front door. We walked on, a few raindrops beginning to spatter down around us, the pavement soon like giraffe skin. We turned up towards our road and then stopped to get our coats out of our bags. Milly had left hers at school, though, so we hurried on, raindrops hitting us in the face because we were walking into the wind. When a few more came, Milly stopped, looked at me. And then we RAN. It was a good idea, but too late, because then it REALLY started, huge ticks leaping up from the pavement, hammering off the parked cars. Soon there were more ticks than a teacher would give in a lifetime and I could barely see.

Milly grabbed my arm. 'In here!' she cried, dragging me off to the left.

She meant the corner shop. I didn't think we needed to go in because we weren't that far from home – but Milly was already running towards the shiny windows. Before I could stop her, she'd shoved the door open,

Mr Hájek's buzzer sounding when she trod on the rubber mat just inside. I followed as Mr Hájek looked up from his counter.

'Hello, girls!' he called out.

'Hello!' we replied, as we wiped our faces with our hands. I took my coat off and hung it on the back of a shopping basket.

'How's the ice hockey, Mr Hájek?' Milly asked.

Mr Hájek loves ice hockey. He supports the Czech Republic and watches them on a little TV beneath his till. Today, he said, the Czech Republic were playing Romania and it was going well.

'Voráček,' he said. 'He's really slapping it. That puck is flying!'

I had no idea what he was talking about, though Milly seemed to get it.

'Voráček's frying,' she said.

Mr Hájek leaned forward and frowned. 'Frying?'

'It means great,' I explained. 'In her language. "Frying" is a new one. She must have learned it in the playground today.'

Mr Hájek smiled and he and Milly chatted, while I moved off towards the sweets aisle. I held my bag in front of me, trying not to let it drip on my skirt as I unzipped the side pocket. I knew there was some change in there – from International Evening last term. Mum had given us two pounds each and I hadn't spent mine. I save up for things, unlike Milly who splurges any money she gets. I probably had a whole pound in there and I was going to spend fifty pence – on Milly. There's no doubt that she's annoying, but she had got my clothes out for me that morning. And, after the day I'd had, I wanted to visit a different room inside myself, one where I could be kind and generous.

I scrabbled around in the front pocket, about to grab a twenty-pence piece, when light blasted in through Mr Hájek's window. The rain had stopped and the sun had come out, yellow light singing off the wet road and all the cars. I was amazed that it had turned bright so quickly and I held a hand up to the glare, though it soon vanished.

'Ah,' Mr Hájek said. 'Sorry, Milly, this chat has been both "frying" and "radical", but I'm going to have to "leave you on read" now. A delivery.'

I thought that it must have been a cloud that had blocked out the sun – but it wasn't. It was a van. It had pulled up right outside Mr Hájek's shop. I looked at it for a second, until my eyes were caught by something else.

And it was so amazing that I dropped my bag, my pencil case coming out of the open pocket, all the change I'd been looking for skittering across the floor beneath Mr Hájek's fridge units.

CHAPTER TWENTY-THREE

Cymbeline

So it WAS a fake. The medal at Hall Place!

The fact that I was right made me clench my fists with satisfaction. Though it annoyed me too. I wanted to go back. I wanted to tell that helper AND Veronique. I wanted to show them the medal as it looked on the Internet. Veronique was asleep, though. And, when we got up in the morning, I couldn't get her on her own.

Because she was practically GLUED to Ellen.

'What do you have for breakfast?' I heard Ellen ask her, as I waited outside the bathroom. They'd been in there for HOURS and I was DESPERATE.

'Weetabix,' Veronique said. 'Normally.'

'So do I!' Ellen cried, though that was a LIE! When

they FINALLY came out, I hissed, 'You have rice crispies.'

'*What?*'

'Yesterday you did NOT have Weetabix. I had Weetabix. ME! YOU had rice crispies!'

Ellen just laughed, and Veronique squinted at me. 'Cymbeline,' she said, 'you're so funny sometimes.'

I watched them hurry off downstairs.

I wanted to tell Veronique about the medal when we were on the way to school – Ellen wouldn't be there, would she? Veronique's mum came, though, with some school clothes for her. She then drove us both and I couldn't get a word in. I just had to listen as Veronique went 'ELLEN this' and 'ELLEN that', babbling on about what a great time they'd had and if she could go to Ellen's gymnastics club.

'And can Ellen come over to our house sometime?'

'Course,' Veronique's mum said. 'I like your hair by the way. Will you do mine like that?'

'Ellen did it,' Veronique replied. 'She's amazing!'

I stared out of the window. '*S-h-e's a-m-a-z-i-n-g*,' I mouthed.

I gave up on the medal for now – because a thought had come to me. And it was BAD. What if Ellen didn't stop at stealing Veronique from me? What if she then moved on to Lance?! What if I had to watch her trying to get him to teach her kick-ups? Or what if she asked to go cycling with him, which Lance loves but I'm not that fussed about (I mean, HILLS, people). Or worse: what if I had to watch them both, knee-deep in Lego, MY Lego, Ellen smirking up at me as they built a brand-new Death Star?!

No. I couldn't let it happen. So I asked Veronique's mum about their burglary. That finally stopped Veronique talking about Ellen, because she wanted to know too. Mrs Chang sighed.

'They really made a mess.'

'Did they pull all the books off the shelves and stuff?'

'That's right. Looking for money, I guess.'

'What did they take?'

'My laptop and David's camera.'

She meant Veronique's dad. 'Was Veronique's room bad?'

'Awful.'

'And they smashed your door down?'

'They did, but it's odd.'

'What is?'

'Well, your Auntie Mill's got CCTV.'

I knew that. My Auntie Mill lives next door to Veronique and I've seen their security cameras.

'It just about stretches to our door, but Mill says she can't see the burglars going in.'

'Can't she?'

'No.'

'So how can they have smashed the door?'

'No idea, though they did. Anyway, it's all cleared up now. Including your room, sweetheart.'

Veronique's mum turned to Veronique and smiled again, patting the top of her plaits.

When we got to school, Veronique hurried towards the gate. She likes to get into class early so she can read. I called out but she didn't hear, so I hitched my bag on my back.

'Bye, Cymbeline.'

'Thanks, Mrs Chang,' I said.

And I thought about what she'd told me – the CCTV didn't show the burglars going in. It didn't make ANY sense, though it reminded me of what the police had said at our house. They'd gone round to all the neighbours and asked if anyone had seen our burglars either coming in, or running away. But no one had. I didn't know what that meant, but I was convinced of one thing – it WAS the same burglars. It had to be.

But did it mean anything?

I didn't know but I HAD to find out – and about the Phoenix Medal. Because, if I did, Veronique would DEFINITELY be interested. And, if she was, then MAYBE she would notice that I existed again.

But how could I find out about either thing? I had no idea until I glanced up at our classroom window. And I nodded to myself because I, Cymbeline Igloo, had come up with a PLAN.

CHAPTER TWENTY-FOUR

Jessica

'Jess!' Milly called from the counter. 'What is it?'

I didn't answer. I just stared through the window, past the message board with people's lost cats on, or sofas for sale. I was staring at the bin right outside Mr Hájek's shop. It was full and sopping wet, some dripping crisp packets poking out next to a soggy pizza box.

They weren't what had caught my eye, though.

Still ignoring Milly, I hurried over to the door, Mr Hájek marching out to get his delivery. I followed him, my right foot hovering over a big puddle. I managed to avoid it and then I was standing on the pavement.

Staring – at Mr Goldy!

He was in the bin! He was wedged beneath the

pizza box, the end of one of his little legs just visible beside a crushed drinks can. The leg was soaking wet and I shook my head, thinking what a REALLY HARD LIFE he was having – before frowning. Because the lady – Mrs Rose – had said she was desperate to get Mr Goldy back! So why had she thrown him away?! It was almost impossible to take in, but then it got even harder. Because, after I'd reached for the leg and pulled, I realised that I'd made a bit of an assumption, probably because I couldn't see much of the teddy.

It wasn't Mr Goldy at all!

It was a different teddy completely!

What?

For a second I just stood there, questions jangling in my head. The first thing I felt was disappointment: I thought I'd found Mr Goldy again. Then I was just amazed. I'd never even found ONE teddy before, but now I'd found TWO in a week. And neither in the best of states! I shook my head, wondering what it meant, about to ask Milly when I stopped again.

Because – now that I was staring at it – I knew this teddy . . .

It was MINE!

And not just THAT – I'd actually made it at the

Build-A-Bear Workshop where we'd gone for Anisa's birthday (she's in my class)! It lives at the end of my bed, but was now in my hand, drenched and mucky, after I'd pulled it out of a bin! And the weirdness didn't even stop there because it was damaged. It hadn't just been shoved in a bin but cut open, its stuffing poking out. You don't really like to think of what's inside your teddies, but I had to because it was right there in front of me as, suddenly, was Milly. She'd come out of the shop and was staring at the teddy too, though she didn't look shocked exactly, or even excited. Or even just a little surprised.

She looked *guilty*!

'Jess,' she said, before staring down at her soggy shoes. 'There's something I've got to tell you.'

CHAPTER TWENTY-FIVE

Cymbeline

My plan was this: I was going to tell Miss Phillips about the Phoenix Medal. That it was a fake! I was going to get her to go on Google, on the big screen, in front of everyone, and bring up the image I'd found. We could then compare it to my drawing! Miss Phillips would be fascinated, and anything that got a teacher going would be sure to excite Veronique.

But it didn't happen.

When I got upstairs, Lance stopped me at the coat pegs. He said that he had some 'grave news'.

'Miss Phillips is on a course,' he said.

'What?' I sighed. 'So we've got . . .'

'A supply teacher. And . . .'

'No. NO!'

'It's Mr Gorton,' Lance said.

And, though he does like to wind me up sometimes, Lance was actually telling the truth. Waiting inside the classroom was, indeed, Mr Gorton, who can be compared to some of the world's most EVIL villains. He even has his own catchphrase to make your blood run cold like Darth Vader when he says, 'Bring them to me now!' Mr Gorton's is scarier than that, though, and it even beats 'Exterminate!' (the Daleks) and 'My Precious!' (Gollum). He sits up straight like there's a drawing pin on his seat and says, 'BE QUIET!'

And, if you've ever heard it, you'll know the effect it has. And the effect of seeing him in the classroom was to puncture my plan like a balloon. There was no point telling *him*. He'd just order me to sit down. I tried explaining it to Lance instead, but he wasn't interested at ALL. He just banged on about the Death Star.

'Steal all Mabel's unicorns!' he said. 'The Lego ones.'

'Uni-legs.'

'What?'

'That's what she calls them now. Uni-legs.'

'So? Who cares? Bring them round to my house!'

I told Lance that I'd try – but how could I? Mabel had put the Uni-legs up in the boxroom, *and* told me all their names. How could I steal Star Spangle? Or little Moon Fizz? Not to mention Sprinkle Love, Tooty Fruits or Rainbow Toes? They were just babies. They hadn't even been given their magic horns yet.

I turned from Lance to Veronique. She was stuck in *A Tale of Two Cities*, though, and you DON'T interrupt Veronique when she's reading. I walked over to Charles Dickens instead. He saw me coming and swam up to the wall of his tank, his mouth opening and closing as if he was trying to tell me something.

'What is it?' I whispered.

But Charles Dickens moved off towards his little treasure chest and then Mr Gorton told me to sit down.

I *tried* talking to Veronique at lunchtime. What were we going to do about the fake?! Before I could get to her, though, Vi told her that her hair looked wicked. Daisy agreed and they all went off together. Five minutes later, they were in the playground doing different styles on each other. It actually, well, looked kind of fun. I like art, as I've said, and this was just another sort really. I even thought about asking to join in, but I wasn't quite brave enough. I played football instead, with Lance and Billy, thinking I might be able to see Veronique at last play. She was off doing something in the Craft Zone, though. I DID see her at home time – but she just shrugged.

'Who knows how many white roses there were?' she said. 'Or red ones?'

I stared at her. 'What do you mean?'

'Well, I didn't look *that* closely. I just believed what you said.'

I nearly argued but there was no point – Veronique hates being wrong. Getting sneered at by that helper must have really affected her. I tried to get her interested in the burglaries instead, but she shrugged *again*.

'Maybe it was the same people. What does it matter? There's nothing we can do about it. Can you give this to Ellen, though?'

Veronique held out an envelope and went off to her dad. I resisted accidently letting it fall in a gutter on the way home, and handed it over.

'What IS it?' Mabel demanded (we were in the kitchen). Ellen grinned.

'Oh, look,' she said, after she'd torn the envelope open. 'A friendship bracelet. We said we'd make them for each other. Tell Veronique I'll give her hers on Friday.'

'Friday?'

'When I go for a SLEEPOVER.'

Ellen's grin grew even wider as she tied the bracelet on to her wrist.

'ELLEN'S GOING TO VERONIQUE'S FOR A SLEEPOVER!' bellowed Mabel, as she jumped up and down.

That week passed so

S

      L

         O

            W

               L

                  Y.

We had Mr Gorton the WHOLE time, though even he wasn't as bad as home. The Squeaky Chicks now felt like maggots eating my brain. Mum and Dad went from arguing to making each other laugh, and then back to arguing again. There was nothing in between.

Mr Fells knocked on the door SIX times to complain about the noise. I had two more dreams about earthquakes (Dad was back in my room) and then one in which I was Chicken Licken and the house fell on my head. That wasn't Dad's fault, though. Stephan came back from work on Wednesday and brought a stepladder inside. He got a saw out, climbed the ladder – and cut a hole in the landing ceiling!

A cloud of dust curled down into my bedroom and we all began to cough. Then Stephan disappeared, his legs vanishing into the roof space, as if a monster was eating him. I stared up until he reappeared and climbed down.

'Bit cramped now in this house, isn't it?'

I nodded – there was no denying it. And it was getting worse. Dad didn't just snore, he left his stuff ALL OVER my bedroom. Shoes, jeans, shirts. Honestly, he is SO UNTIDY.

'But what's that got to do with you going up there?'

'Because we're getting two extra bedrooms. And another loo.'

'You're going to lift up beds and stuff?' I craned my neck to the black hole.

'No! We've had the plan for ages. We were never

going to just move in. This squash is only temporary. We're going to do a loft conversion.'

'Today?'

'It'll take a few months. We'll have to take the whole roof off the house first.'

I stared after Stephan as he called Mum up, then held the stepladder for her so that she could have a look.

'But I like our roof,' I said.

Mum and Stephan tried to convince me that the loft conversion would solve all our problems, but no end of new rooms could have made Ellen any better. I had to avoid the living room because she practised her gymnastics in there. I went in once and got booted in the face by a cartwheel. We ran out of milk THREE more times that week because she glugged it, and she ALWAYS beat me to the biscuit tin. Not that she admitted anything.

'I did NOT eat the chocolate ones!' she insisted after I'd found YET ANOTHER mound of digestive crumbs. I said she MUST have, but Mum said that I had to believe her – otherwise I'd be calling her a liar. I wanted to say that she WAS a liar! Something told me that Ellen was actually telling the truth, though, even if it wasn't the *whole* truth. So, when she was watching TV, I snuck up the stairs. *V-e-r-y q-u-i-e-t-l-y*, I pulled the door of the boxroom open and, trying not to knock any Uni-legs over, I searched EVERY-WHERE. The drawers, behind the books, in Ellen's schoolbag. But there was nothing, at least not until I was about to give up. I took a last look at the room – and froze. There was a bulge at the far end of Ellen's blow-up mattress! And, when I lifted it up, what do you think I found?

WELL?

YES!

There were:

Three chocolate Hobnobs.
Nine chocolate digestives.
Sixteen Jaffa Cakes.
And forty-seven chocolate fingers!

FORTY-
SEVEN!

And that wasn't all. There were ALSO three of my Subbuteo men – which I'd been missing – and NOT MR FLUFFY!

'MUM!' I bellowed.

Mum came running and I held the mattress up, expecting her to be outraged. Her eyes would go as big as footballs! Her hands would fly to her hips – like they did when Dad turned up! She'd say,

'Well!'

and stomp downstairs, calling Ellen

'Young lady'

before demanding that Ellen come upstairs to give her

'AN EXPLANATION'.

I felt the first actual happiness I'd had in ages – but it faded. Because, when Mum appeared in the doorway, and I pointed to the stash, she *didn't* look angry.

She looked sad!

'Cymbeline,' she said, glancing behind her before

pushing the door to. And then she told me that, instead of being cross with Ellen, I should try to U-N-D-E-R-S-T-A-N-D her.

'WHAT?!'

Ellen, Mum said, was going through a 'difficult phase'. She was finding it 'hard to adjust'. She was joining a new family and living in a new house. And she missed her mum.

'Why doesn't she go and live with her then?'

'Because she lives with Stephan. He's her primary carer. And Stephan's living with us now.'

'But can't she go and stay with her mum for a night or two?'

'Yes, and she will, but not now. Her mum's away and anyway we want to have a long period together so we can all get used to . . .'

'Her stealing my things? And squashed Jaffa Cakes? Broken chocolate fingers? I'm eating these by the way. ALL of them.'

'No!' Mum sighed. 'Get used to being *together*. As a *new family*. I never realised it would be so . . .'

But Mum didn't finish her sentence because she did something else. She started to cry, which made me feel terrible, as if it was MY FAULT. As if it was me who was behaving like a chocolate-obsessed squirrel! When Mum calmed down, she turned to me.

'Least you'll get some space from each other on Friday.'

'Yes,' I hissed. 'Because she's going round for a sleepover at MY best friend's house. Isn't she?'

And I grabbed Not Mr Fluffy, pushed past Mum and ran off to my room.

That made me even more guilty because I knew it would make Mum feel worse, though it still wasn't my fault. Mum SO should have punished Ellen! The chocolate biscuits were one thing, but hiding Not Mr Fluffy from me? Mum should have seen how bad that was, especially as she knew how I'd felt after losing my original !Teddy of Most Extreme Importance! – Mr Fluffy. I sat on my bed, waiting for her knock on the door, determined just to sit there and ignore it.

But I nodded to myself and told Mum to come in.

Because suddenly, and without meaning to, I, Cymbeline Igloo, had come up with ANOTHER PLAN.

And this one was going to work.

CHAPTER TWENTY-SIX

Cymbeline

'Mum,' I said, when her blotchy face appeared round the door. 'Ellen's going to Veronique's, right?' Mum nodded. 'But what are WE doing on Friday?'

'After school d'you mean? I'm not sure. We could . . .'

'No,' I said. 'During the day.'

Mum blinked at me. 'Well, the same as usual. School.'

'But what about the elections?'

'The . . . ?'

'Council elections?'

'Aren't elections normally on Thursdays?'

'Miss Phillips said yes, but not this year. Something to do with the extra bank holiday. What will we be doing?'

Mum frowned. 'Well, if they are on Friday, voting. At least I will be. And whoever finally promises to get a pelican crossing put in on that junction will get my . . .'

'But where will you be voting?' I asked.

And her face froze. Now Mum is, as you may know, quite forgetful. She has, in the past, forgotten loads of school things, including trips, World Book Days, International Evenings, parents' evenings, sports tournaments, packed lunches for sports tournaments that she'd actually remembered, PE kits, Inset Days and even, once, the start of term. What she'd forgotten now was that, on Friday, our school was going to be a polling station – which meant that it would be SHUT all day! Horror crept over her face as she wondered how she was going to look after me.

She spun round and I followed her downstairs, watching as she grabbed her phone off the kitchen worktop. She swiped into her diary and mumbled silent prayers, before her face collapsed in relief. I've told you that she teaches art now – well, her school was closed for the elections too.

'Thank you, God,' she said, as Ellen came in to find out what the fuss was about. She looked guilty (having clearly guessed that we'd found her secret stash). But I didn't mention that.

'Is your school a polling station on Friday?'

'Dunno,' Ellen said.

'Well, let's see, shall we? Mum, can you check?'

And Mum went on her phone – then shook her head. Ellen pointed at me. 'So HE doesn't have to go to school on Friday, but I DO?'

'Yes,' Mum said, with a wince. Then she added, 'Sorr-ee, love,' though my response was a little different.

I did not apologise. Instead, I said,

HA! HA! HA! HA! HA! HA! HA! HA! HA! HA! HA!
HA! HA! HA! HA! HA! HA! HA! HA! HA! HA! HA!
HA! HA! HA! HA! HA! HA! HA! HA! HA! HA! HA!
HA! HA! HA! HA! HA! HA! HA! HA! HA! HA! HA!
HA! HA! HA! HA! HA! HA! HA! HA! HA! HA! HA!
HA! HA! HA! HA! HA! HA! HA! HA! HA! HA! HA!
HA! HA! HA! HA! HA! HA! HA! HA! HA! HA! HA!
HA! HA! HA! HA! HA! HA! HA! HA! HA! HA! HA!
HA! HA! HA! HA! HA! HA! HA! HA! HA! HA! HA!
HA! HA! HA! HA! HA! HA! HA! HA! HA! HA! HA!
HA! HA! HA! HA! HA! HA! HA! HA! HA! HA! HA!
HA! HA! HA! HA! HA! HA! HA! HA! HA! HA! HA!
HA! HA! HA! HA! HA! HA! HA! HA! HA! HA! HA!
HA! HA! HA! HA! HA! HA! HA! HA! HA! HA! HA!
HA! HA! HA! HA! HA! HA! HA! HA! HA! HA! HA!
HA! HA! HA! HA! HA! HA! HA! HA! HA! HA! HA!
HA! HA! HA! HA! HA! HA! HA! HA! HA! HA! HA!
HA! HA! HA! HA! HA! HA! HA! HA! HA! HA! HA!
HA! HA! HA! HA! HA! HA! HA! HA! HA! HA! HA!
HA! HA! HA! HA! HA! HA! HA! HA! HA! HA! HA!
HA! HA! HA! HA! HA! HA! HA! HA! HA! HA! HA!
HA! HA! HA! HA! HA! HA! HA! HA! HA! HA! HA!
HA! HA! HA! HA! HA! HA! HA! HA! HA! HA! HA!

HA! HA! HA! HA! HA! HA! HA! HA! HA! HA! HA!
HA! HA! HA! HA! HA! HA! HA! HA! HA! HA! HA!
HA! HA! HA! HA! HA! HA! HA! HA! HA! HA! HA!
HA! HA! HA! HA! HA! HA! HA! HA! HA! HA! HA!
HA! HA! HA! HA! HA! HA! HA! HA! HA! HA! HA!
HA! HA! HA! HA!

HA!

'So,' Mum said, after Ellen had stomped out (good riddance), 'shall we *do* something on Friday? In the daytime?'

'Great!'

'Any ideas?'

'Oh yes!' I said. And I told Mum my plan.

Mum poked her tongue into her cheek and nodded.

'Okay, sure. And I think Stephan would like that. Shall I see if he can get a day off work? It would be really good if you two could spend some more time together.'

'Hmmm,' I said, pretending to consider this. '*Maaay-beee*. Though I was thinking that, instead of Stephan, perhaps we could take . . .'

And I was about to tell Mum the LAST bit of my plan. But I stopped: the doorbell had rung and I ran right past her to answer it.

'Hi, Dad!' I said.

CHAPTER TWENTY-SEVEN

Jessica

'But why didn't you grab one of YOUR teddies?' I hissed, after Milly had told me what she'd done.

'I couldn't! I don't care about teddies, do I? I've only got two and I don't even know where they are! I didn't have time to look for them!'

'You had time to grab one of mine, didn't you?! And shove it in a plastic bag?' I glared at Milly and then turned to my teddy, prodding its stuffing back in with my index finger and then trying to squeeze its chest together.

'But my teddies don't look like teddies,' Milly insisted. 'One's a frog. The other one's a dinosaur.'

'So? You could have given her one of those, couldn't you?!'

'No! The lady would have known. As soon as she looked at it, she would have come straight back. This way, if she did open the bag, we could insist that *that* was the teddy we'd found in the river. Anyway, you've got your teddy back now, haven't you?'

'Yeah, all ripped open.'

'So what? Stop being salty.'

'Salty?'

'Annoyed. Look, Mum'll fix it. You don't have to tell her how it happened. Anyway, Jess, you're ignoring the most wig thing!'

'Wig?!'

'Important!'

'What important thing?'

Milly looked at me like I was stupid. 'Well, I gave the woman *that* teddy, didn't I, pretending it was the one we found at Cuckmere Haven? Which means . . .'

And it hit me. Of course! I was still mad with Milly for sacrificing one of my teddies, BUT WE STILL HAD MR GOLDY! So now I was even more cross at the fact that she hadn't told me.

'Where IS he?' I demanded, grabbing Milly by both arms.

Milly showed me after I'd marched her home. Mum

had said we might have to let ourselves in, but Dad was there. He'd just been to pick up Benji and he looked a lot better than he had that morning. He said hi and asked if we wanted a snack.

'In a minute,' I said. 'We're just going to—'

'Get changed,' Milly said.

And we ran upstairs. Milly put a chair under the door handle so that Benji couldn't get in.

'Come on then,' I said. 'Get him out.'

Milly shook her head. 'No, see if you can find him first.'

She was clearly expecting that to be difficult – but it wasn't. She'd hidden Mr Goldy behind some books on the top shelf (by standing on her desk). You could see something was wrong because all the Secret Sevens were sticking out too far. I was madder than MAD. 'That wasn't very hard,' I spat. 'You *said* he was safe. Why didn't you tell me?'

'But he is safe,' Milly protested. 'Benji can't get up there!'

'But what about Mum? When she's cleaning? We told her we gave the teddy back, didn't we?'

'Chill. She thinks we have.'

'Yes, but if she spots him we'll be in trouble. Or,

worse, she'll just shove him on my bed with all the others where Benji'll see him. He could do anything!'

'So where *should* we keep him?' Milly asked, finally looking a bit sorry.

I climbed up on her desk, grabbed Mr Goldy and cast my eyes round the room. Every single place looked wrong – until I saw our old doll's house. Mum only ever cleans the outside of it. Benji might look in it because he does like playing with the dolls sometimes, though his current dinosaur obsession meant that he hadn't for a while. I was umming and aahing, though not for long – there were footsteps on the stairs. I lifted the roof off, stuffed Mr Goldy in, then just got it back down before the door rattled.

Mum was home.

'Not bad,' she said, after Milly had taken the chair away. She scanned the room like I had. I stared right at her, trying to keep my eyes away from the doll's house.

'Bad?'

'Tidy, I mean. Though can you pick up your dressing gowns and pyjamas, please? And put those piles of washing away?'

'Can't we do it later?'

'Now, please. We've . . .'

'Yes, Mum?'

'There's a man coming round.'

'From the council?'

'What?'

'You know, to do an assessment? The modifications?'

'Right. Er, yes. Five minutes, please.'

We shrugged and did tidy up, though why the council man had to come again and look in our room, I didn't know. When we'd finished, Mum said we should have a run-around in the park. Dad pushed Benji along there too and sat on a bench (not kicking a ball with Benji like he normally did). We all went on the climbing frames. When we got back, the council man was just leaving. He was different from the last one – really smiley, in a shiny-looking suit. He shook Mum's hand and gave her a big, glossy leaflet. Mum didn't look happy. Maybe he'd suggested even more expensive things. She smiled quickly when she saw us, though, and hugged us all.

'Had a good day?' she asked.

I nodded. It had been awful at school, but knowing that Mr Goldy was upstairs was brilliant. I smiled to myself, though doing that made me feel bad. I frowned at that before understanding why. I'd had a thought and it was one I really should have had before. I wanted to know if Milly was thinking it too and I took her down the garden, telling Mum we were going to feed Boffo.

'He must have been really special,' I whispered.

'Mr Goldy? He is special.'

'I know.' I tipped some pellets into Boffo's bowl, though he didn't really need any. 'But special for the kid who lost him. Their granny took a lot of trouble to find him, didn't she?'

'So what?' Milly held a carrot out to Boffo, who sniffed it. 'They shouldn't have dropped him in a river, should they?'

I knew that was true and I nodded: but maybe it wasn't the owner kid's fault that Mr Goldy had got lost (whenever that happened). In any case, it was weird to think of someone out there, missing him. I'd missed him for the last few days and I'd hardly had him any time at all. It was also weird to think that, of course, they didn't call him Mr Goldy (though that SO was his name).

What DID they call him? Was it one of the names we'd thought of giving him?

Mr Cuddles perhaps?

I'd probably never know. Whatever it was, I just hoped that whoever *had* owned him wasn't going through any big problems, any upheavals in their life, which would mean that they could have really done with him right then.

And then I had another thought. Milly had given the lady – Mrs Rose – the teddy in a plastic bag. When Mrs Rose opened it, did she know that the teddy *wasn't* Mr Goldy. If so, why didn't she bring it back to us? Why did she throw it away in Mr Hájek's bin?

And why did she cut it open first?

That was really weird.

What kind of a granny would do *that*?

CHAPTER TWENTY-EIGHT

Jessica

That question really bugged me – all through supper, during which I could have throttled Milly. She kept asking Benji if he was sure that he was only into dinosaurs at the moment – and not dolls. She kept saying that she thought dolls were rubbish and that there was no point playing with them. I cut glances at her, which just about kept her quiet, and Benji didn't seem to notice anything. I went back to thinking about Mrs Rose, and I was still doing that at bedtime.

After Mum had kissed us both goodnight (and we'd had secret cuddles with Mr Goldy), I kept seeing Mrs Rose's face. That Cheshire Cat smile, which she'd held on to for too long. The way she looked at us. I remembered the way she'd snatched the bag from Milly and hurried away. When I thought about it, she hadn't looked relieved to get a kid's teddy back. No. She'd looked gleeful. Excited.

But about what?

I didn't know the answer and I just couldn't put the question aside. The way I'd felt about Dad that morning came back to me and that didn't help either. I couldn't get to sleep and, when I did, I woke up again. I stared into the swirling darkness and thought about finding Mr Goldy, and cleaning him, and how Mum had put him on WhatsApp. Mrs Rose had got back to Mum REALLY quickly. It was almost like she'd been waiting for someone to find the teddy. I pictured her taking it out of its plastic bag near Mr Hájek's shop and seeing the teddy Milly had substituted. *Did* she know it was the wrong one? Or did she really think that it *was* the teddy we'd found at Cuckmere Haven?

There was only one way of finding out: by comparing my Build-A-Bear teddy to Mr Goldy. Though was the picture of Mr Goldy – which Mrs Rose would have seen on WhatsApp – still on Mum's phone?

I sat up. I could only just make Milly out in the

darkness, but I knew she was asleep. Keeping my eyes on the strip of light beneath our door, I got out of bed and tiptoed past her. On the landing I could see okay because Mum and Dad keep the bathroom light on at night. The first thing I looked for was light from under their door, but there was nothing. Downstairs was dark too, and silent, but for a distant, soft humming. It was probably the fridge and I headed towards it, knowing that Mum's phone would be charging in the kitchen, because she doesn't like to leave it in her bedroom at night.

The kitchen was dark but for the clock on the front of the cooker. The humming I'd heard *was* the fridge – and it gave me an idea. Not wanting to turn the kitchen light on, I pulled the fridge door open, a wedge of chilly yellow immediately making me shiver. It spread out towards the breakfast bar, though, where ghostly-looking cereal packets and bowls stood waiting for the morning, like a sleeping city. Mum's phone was next to them, sitting on the leaflet – more like a big brochure, really – that she'd been given earlier.

Leaving the fridge door open, I stepped over and picked Mum's phone up. Using the fridge light to see by, I tapped in Mum's PIN, the screen then showing a photo of us: Dad, Milly, Benji and me, all huddled together, grinning. Or most of us were. Milly was sticking her tongue out and it made me feel warm inside, though not as much as seeing Dad. He looked really well and I thought about him earlier, all cheerful when we got back from school. Such a relief. I smiled and then searched the screen for the photos icon.

It was in the top-right corner. I tapped it and yes – the picture of Mr Goldy WAS still there. I studied it but not for long because I needed my other teddy to compare. I'd given it to Mum earlier and she'd put it on top of her sewing box. I turned towards the living room to fetch it, but stopped. The teddy was there, in the kitchen. It was sitting in my place, waiting for me.

Because Mum had already mended it.

Mum had looked so tired before. She had another shift in the morning, but she'd taken the time to sew my teddy up. I sighed and glanced over towards the stairs, feeling very still inside as I set the teddy back down and picked up Mum's phone again.

And I saw that the teddies weren't really like each other.

Mr Goldy's face was round – but my other one had

a pointy nose. Mr Goldy was REALLY fluffy and mine WASN'T. I frowned, wondering again why Mrs Rose hadn't just come back and asked for the right one! Unable to work it out, I blinked, my eyes falling on the brochure that Mum's phone had been sitting on.

And Mrs Rose went out of my mind.

The brochure was supposed to be an information thing – about how to make your home easier for someone with MS. To begin with, I thought it was that because there were houses on the cover. But there was also a name printed in big letters across the front.

Fox & Sons.

I'd seen that name. It was on boards all over town. Outside people's houses. Using the phone light, I opened the brochure and swallowed: because there were more houses inside, underneath a heading that announced Properties For Sale.

What?

Was this the brochure Mum had been given? Yes, I recognised it. I flicked through the rest of the pages and saw more houses, all for sale, but NOTHING about modifications. So the man who'd come round earlier WASN'T from the council? No. He can't have been. Mum had only *said* that.

He was an estate agent.

And that could only mean ONE THING.

We were going to sell our house.

CHAPTER TWENTY-NINE

Cymbeline

That week I LONGED for Friday to come.

First, however, I had to deal with the worst Wednesday and the most hideous Thursday in HISTORY! Why so bad? Because even more visitors came to stay in our overstuffed house. It was Mabel who brought them, though at first I didn't realise. I was on the sofa, with Mum, in a rare moment of peace. We were watching *The Simpsons* when Mum turned to me.

'What are you doing?' she said.

'Doing?' I hadn't realised I'd been doing anything. But Mum stared at me.

'You're scratching your head.'

'So?' I turned back to Bart and Homer. 'It's itchy and scratchy.'

Mum frowned. '*How* itchy and scratchy?'

I said it was pretty much TOTALLY itchy and scratchy, actually, and Mum groaned.

'I thought we were done with those!'

'Those?'

'Nits,' she exclaimed. 'Head lice. Now I think of it, Mabel's been scratching too. Come on!'

And I had to stop watching *The Simpsons* and go up to the bathroom. Mum washed my hair and again I wished I was a Tudor, only getting this once a year. Mum's done this loads of times, though she still managed to get LOADS of soap in my eyes.

'That's your fault! For wriggling.'

'But I always wriggle,' I said. 'How come you haven't got used to it by now?!'

After that, she made the hair washing pointless anyway, because she practically yanked it all out with this evil steel comb. She showed me all the creepy-crawlies she'd found and there were loads of them – all from Mabel. And they'd been living there, scurrying about and laying eggs, on MY head! The idea was DISGUSTING, as if my head was some sort of nit hotel. My only consolation was that Ellen and Mabel had to have their hair done too.

Though NOTHING could make up for what happened on Thursday night. So, if you found the nits revolting, I'd advise you to skip the next bit.

On Thursday night I was getting ready for bed – excited about the next day. But I started feeling itchy again, and this time it wasn't my head.

It was *somewhere else*.

Mabel started it. We were in the bathroom, cleaning our teeth, only she was cleaning hers with one hand and scratching herself (*somewhere else*) with the other. When Ellen came in to clean her teeth, I saw that she was scratching herself too (*somewhere else*). And that made me want to scratch myself (*somewhere else*). I did, and Mum saw us all doing it. And she took me off into my bedroom.

'Cym,' she said, 'I'm . . .'

'Yes, Mum?'

'Going to have to check your bottom.'

I stared at her. 'My . . . ?'

'Bottom, Cym. It's itching, isn't it?'

'Probably just sore. From football.'

'I don't think so. It's probably Mabel again.'

'What is?'

But Mum didn't answer. She just knelt down behind me and pulled my PJs down. Then she said, 'Yes, thought so.'

'You thought what?'

'Well, it's . . . worms.'

'WORMS?!'

'Yes. Mabel probably brought them . . .'

'Wait!' I said, not really able to believe what I was hearing. 'You're telling me that you can *see worms*?'

'Er, yes.'

'In my bottom?'

'Yes. Nematode worms. Though not in. I can't look in your bottom, obviously. They're more . . .'

'What? WHAT, MUM?'

'Crawling out,' she said.

'THERE ARE WORMS CRAWLING OUT OF MY BOTTOM?!!!!!!!!!!! BECAUSE OF MABEL?!!!!!'

'Yes,' Mum said. 'I'm sorry to say that there are.'

And she made me put pants on before forcing me to drink this DISGUSTING yellow liquid.

'Night, Thimbeline!' said Mabel ten minutes later.

I slammed my bedroom door. Then I got into bed, the following thought hammering through my brain until I was asleep.

THERE ARE WORMS CRAWLING OUT
OF MY BOTTOM . . .

THERE ARE WORMS CRAWLING OUT
OF MY BOTTOM . . .

THERE ARE WORMS CRAWLING OUT OF
MY BOTTOM . . .

THERE ARE WORMS CRAWLING OUT OF
MY BOTTOM . . .

THERE ARE WORMS CRAWLING OUT OF
MY BOTTOM . . .

THERE ARE WORMS CRAWLING OUT OF MY
BOTTOM . . .

THERE ARE WORMS CRAWLING OUT OF MY BOTTOM
. . .

THERE ARE WORMS CRAWLING OUT OF MY BOTTOM
. . .

THERE ARE WORMS CRAWLING OUT OF MY BOTTOM
. . .

THERE ARE WORMS CRAWLING OUT OF MY BOTTOM . . .

THERE ARE WORMS CRAWLING OUT OF . . .

THERE ARE WORMS CRAWLING OUT . . .

THERE ARE WORMS CRAWLING . . .

THERE ARE WORMS . . .

...

And they all
look like Mabel.

CHAPTER THIRTY

Cymbeline

On Friday morning, though, I forgot about it because it was polling day.

And, if my plan came off, then this hideous life I'd been living for what seemed like years now would soon be over.

I didn't say anything at breakfast about Dad coming with us to Hall Place. I just stayed in my pyjamas, to demonstrate to Ellen that I was not in ANY sort of hurry that morning (unlike her, ha ha ha, etc.). Stephan chivvied her and Mabel to go and get dressed while I just smiled.

'Have a *gr-e-a-t d-a-y*,' I said, when they were ready. 'At *sch-o-o-o-o-o-o-o-o-o-o-l*.'

'Aren't you sad?' Mabel wondered, as Stephan zipped her coat up. 'School is WONDERFUL.'

'I'll get over it,' I said, before going up to Ellen, whose face was like a plank. 'Here. Take this for your packed lunch. I found some after all.'

I handed her a chocolate finger and then they left for school.

'Right,' Mum said, looking a little nervous for some reason. 'I suppose we'd better get going then, hadn't we?'

I nodded and ran upstairs to wake Dad up. After that, I got dressed and grabbed a bag, sliding my picture of the Phoenix Medal inside. I also stuffed some of my favourite Subbuteo men in, plus Not Mr Fluffy.

'What are you bringing those for?' Mum asked.

'Safety,' I said. I had no idea when we'd be back and whether Ellen would be home before me.

We had to wait for Dad, but eventually he was ready. I thought we'd drive, but Mum said she didn't want to make unnecessary car journeys. I was glad – it meant that we'd have more time together, which we did – on the top deck of the 53. And Dad was SO funny. When the bus stopped in front of us, we clambered up the stairs, me sitting next to Mum, Dad in the seat in front.

'D'you know something about buses, Cym?' he asked, turning round.

'Dunno,' I said. 'What?'

'Well.' Dad looked round at all the seats. 'The bus has wheels. And these wheels, which are ON the bus, go ROUND. They go round and round, round and round. The wheels on the bus go . . .'

'*Dad*,' I said.

'And round and round and round and round. Then they go round and round. Did you know that?'

'*Dad!* Don't be silly . . .'

'And –' he held up a finger – 'that's not all. Sometimes there are babies on the bus. What you may not know is that *they* go, "Wah, wah, wah!" Can you believe that?'

'Dad! That lady can hear you.' I ducked behind him because someone really was looking at us.

'Well, I'm glad because she looks to me like a mummy. And the mummies on the bus do something too. They go, "Nod, nod, nod".'

'This mummy does,' Mum said, trying not to laugh for some reason. I was laughing, though, and so was the lady who'd overheard us. 'What do the Out-of-Work Actors on the bus do?' Mum asked.

'Phone their agents,' Dad said. 'ALL DAY LONG.'

I asked what an agent was, but Dad didn't hear. Instead, he did loads of other people on the bus, including me ('Charlton, Charlton, Charlton'), Mr Fells ('Stop that, stop that, stop that') and Mabel ('Unicorn, unicorn, unicorn').

'What does Stephan do?' I laughed. Dad thought about it.

'He goes, "Hammer! Hammer! Hammer!" And not just all day long. He does it most evenings too.'

I really laughed then because that was SO true, though for some reason Mum didn't get into it. She was being a bit stiff, like she wasn't quite there with us. Or pretending not to be there. She couldn't pretend at Hall Place, though, because when we got there Dad was SPECTACULAR.

The bus dropped us off about ten minutes' walk away. I was in the middle, holding Mum and Dad's hands. My mum and dad split up when I was a baby and I'd never, EVER, not ONCE walked with them like that. It was so GREAT, especially when Dad ran forward and they swung me. After that – and probably because Mum wasn't laughing anyway – Dad stopped being silly. Instead, he pointed out this big bird in an oak tree.

'The one with blue on its wings?'

'That's right, Cym. It's a jay,' Dad said.

Mum frowned. 'Didn't know you were into birds.'

'Played a birdwatcher once,' he explained. 'Had to gen up.'

'Was that on TV?' I asked.

Dad said it was, and told us about all the things he was 'up for' at the moment, the acting jobs that he was hoping to do.

'And if you get in that film,' I asked, 'will you be rich?'

'Minted! What colour yacht shall I buy?'

'Red, because of Charlton. Though it can't be too big.'

'What?! Why not?'

'Because then no one can invade it. It'll just be for us. Make sure there's an art studio for Mum, though.'

'Sure,' Dad said, and he smiled across at Mum, though she bit her lip for some reason, and looked away. After that, he pointed at a robin.

'I know that one!' I said.

'And that's a dog.'

'Dad!'

'And that's a lamp post, in case you were wondering.'

I shook my head and kept hold of both their hands and it was brilliant, though at Hall Place there was a PROBLEM.

There were two coaches outside the big Tudor house and I should have realised what that meant. I didn't until we were standing at reception.

'Sorry,' the man behind the desk said, as Mum was reaching for her purse. 'It's just school visits on Mondays and Fridays.'

'*Really?*'

'It does say on our website.'

Mum sighed. 'We've come a long way, though. Couldn't we just tag on to a school?'

The man looked horrified. 'Insurance,' he said. 'Quite impossible.'

'I am a teacher,' Mum said. 'At a different school, yes, but . . .'

'Sorry. Only official school visits are—'

'But we are here for a school visit,' Dad said.

Mum and I turned to Dad, and so did the man. 'You are?' He looked behind Dad for a line of kids, which obviously wasn't there.

'Indeed,' Dad insisted. 'I'm . . .'

'Yes?'

Dad swallowed. 'Henry the Eighth.'

'You're . . . ?'

'Henry the Eighth. In the . . . story workshop. I'm booked from eleven to one.'

'Booked?'

'Yes,' Dad insisted, before turning to Mum. 'Janet, did you bring the booking confirmation?'

'What?'

'She's forgotten.' Dad sighed. 'My agent. She's new. And this is my son. His school's a polling station today so I've had to bring him along.'

'Right. I see. Well, I need to check.'

The man turned to his computer screen, which I thought would obviously get us thrown out. But Dad did something SO cool. He slid a hand through to the back of the screen while the man wasn't looking, and unplugged it from the rest of the computer! The man frowned.

'Oh!'

'What is it?' Dad asked, his voice all cheerful. 'Have you found me?'

'No. System's gone down. Third time this week.'

'Really?' Dad sighed. 'Technology, eh? Probably the hard drive.'

'The . . . ?'

'Hard drive. Yes. Terrible things, hard drives. Anyway, we'll just mooch around until it's up and running again. This way, is it?' Dad pointed towards the main room where kids in blue jumpers were already filing in.

'Yes. Though . . .'

'Don't worry,' Dad said. 'We can find our way.' And, with that, he drew Mum and me away from the desk and in through the big doors.

'You're outrageous,' Mum hissed, as our feet clomped across the wooden floor.

'You're brilliant!' I said.

Dad tricking us in felt great. I grabbed an activity board from a hook on the wall and told Dad where we needed to start. We went up this narrow back staircase into a room with an amazing tiled ceiling. I was about to tell Dad some of the things I'd learned before, but I didn't need to. He told *us* things.

'The Tudors often had two sleeps,' he said. 'They went to bed really early because it was expensive to light their houses. They'd wake up in the night and do things for a couple of hours, before going back to bed again.' He told us what they ate, and how their clothes had holes in the armpits for the sweat to go through. He knew it all because of a different acting job, though it wasn't on *Horrible Histories* unfortunately. Still, I was dead impressed, though Mum wasn't (or at least she wasn't admitting it). I was annoyed with her. Why couldn't she just get into it? It was so fabulous being here together, but she was being all sniffy with Dad, and suspicious of him, when all he was being was funny. She couldn't resist him for long, though.

'Ah,' the man from the reception said, finding us down in the kitchens. 'There you are. You'd better come along or you'll be late.'

'Late?' Dad said.

'For your workshop.'

'My . . . ?'

'Workshop! Henry the Eighth. Computer's still on the blink and I can't confirm, so we'd better just go ahead. Wouldn't want you to waste the journey. I've spoken to the teachers who are here and fixed it up with them. We've got four schools waiting in the main hall and the fifth are just sitting down. All very excited. Did you bring your own costume, or do you want to use one of ours?'

CHAPTER THIRTY-ONE

Cymbeline

Dad stared at the man and went SO white. The man was obviously waiting for Dad to answer, but he couldn't, so Mum did it for him.

'Fabulous!' she said. 'We'll come right along, won't we? The kids are in for a real treat! It'll be just like going back in time.'

'Excellent. Well, come on then,' said the man.

Dad jerked into life and, with a look of horror on his face, he followed the man out of the room. Mum and I followed too – NO WAY we were missing this – until the man took Dad off into some back rooms. Mum and I went into the main hall again where the kids from the five schools were kneeling on the floor, their different-coloured jumpers making them look like a giant, fidgety flag. It was strange to see them all in uniform and me not, and I felt a bit shy, especially as we didn't sit on the floor but on a couple of chairs at the side. It only lasted a few minutes, though, because Mum suddenly grabbed my arm, her eyes like MOONS as she stared –

At Henry VIII.

Dad had a full costume on: yellow tights, padded trousers, puffy jacket and ginger beard. He jumped on to a little stage, put his hands on his hips and ROARED.

'Bow! I am your king! Bow, you naughty knaves!'

Dad glared at us all and we had no choice: we all scrambled to our feet (adults included) and bowed.

'Now,' Dad said, once we were sitting down again, 'I am going to tell you about my life. You will sit there and be impressed. Meanwhile, I expect your full attention. And that means EVERYONE!'

Dad bellowed the last word out and strode towards the edge of the room where a teacher had snuck her mobile phone out.

'Sorry,' she said, looking a bit scared. Dad nodded as she shoved it into her handbag.

'So,' Dad said, 'I am the King of England, old

Henry's second son. Who can tell me which Henry he was?'

A boy at the front said, 'Seventh?'

'Excellent,' Dad said. 'You are very clever. You can be my Lord Chancellor. You will build a big house like Cardinal Wolsey did, and I will steal it from you. Meanwhile, we are at my palace in Greenwich. My brother Arthur has just died. Cry, you knaves!'

We all cried.

'That's enough. I am king now so you must all be very happy. I have a problem, though. I have a kingdom and many palaces, but I need something else? What?'

A girl put her hand up this time and Dad nodded. 'Yes, my dear?'

'A wee.'

'What? I need a wee?'

'No,' the girl said. 'I do.'

We all waited until the girl came back (she was bright red). Dad asked her again if she knew what HE needed.

'A wife?'

'Indeed! I need a wife. Madam, if you will?'

Dad was still standing near the scared teacher – and he held his hand out. The teacher shrank back and said, 'No way,' – but there was no denying Dad. He turned to the teacher's school.

'You lot, in Yorkist white. Should this maiden be my wife?'

'YES!' they all screamed.

And so, blushing like mad, the teacher let Dad lead her on to the little stage. First he looked her up and down, and then he grimaced.

'What does Adidas mean?' he said, staring at her hoody. Then he just shrugged and did the most embarrassing thing. He started this RIDICULOUS dancing, all round the teacher, which he told us was something called 'courtship'. Then he declared that the teacher was actually Catherine of Aragon and that she had a job to do.

'We are now married. I'm sure you're very pleased. So I want a baby, and I want one FAST. Go over there and have one, please.'

The kids all laughed and the teacher blushed again. She did as she was told, though, scurrying in the direction Dad was pointing, which was actually towards us. Mum lifted up my bag.

'Give her your teddy,' she said. 'For a baby!'

That was a great idea and I pulled out Not Mr

Fluffy. I handed him to the teacher who took him back to Dad. Dad was delighted, but, after he'd pretended to inspect Not Mr Fluffy, his look turned to horror.

'But this is a GIRL!' he said (though Not Mr Fluffy is a boy!). 'Never mind. We shall call it Mary but, Madame, I am not pleased. I probably should have made it clear – I need a BOY baby. Go away and have another one. A BOY this time.'

The teacher, however, shook her head.

'What?' Dad said. 'No boy?'

'Sorry.'

'I see. Well, in that case . . .' Dad stuck his finger out like that man on the telly. 'You're fired! Go and live in a country house somewhere while I find a new wife. Go on, go on!' He shooed the teacher off the stage and then stared round the audience.

'You'll do!' he said.

The teacher Dad was pointing at now was fairly round, and quite old. I expected her to resist – like the first one had – but she was UP for it. She said, 'Yippee!' and skipped up on to the stage. Dad immediately did his prancing again, which was even more hilarious than before. The teacher started acting all coy, though, turning her head away and refusing when Dad puckered his lips up and closed his eyes, clearly wanting a kiss. Dad had to dance even more, shouting out that her beauty was beyond compare – before having an idea. He started to sing 'Greensleeves'. He belted it out in fact, his voice echoing round the big room until the teacher melted. Dad took hold of her hand.

'What's your name?'

'I'm Anne Boleyn,' the teacher said.

'Well, you can Boleyn by having a baby. Off you go then!'

The Anne Boleyn teacher also came in our direction. We'd got Not Mr Fluffy back from the other teacher and Mum handed him over. She took him to Dad, but once again he was livid, screwing his face up like a baby.

'ANOTHER GIRL!' he wailed.

And the whole place cracked up. We laughed even more when Dad rummaged in the dressing-up box I'd seen before, and came out with a plastic sword. He made the teacher kneel down while he cut her head off, all the time saying it was her fault.

'It's these GIRLS,' he hissed. 'They are SO annoying, aren't they, boys?'

All the boys cheered (including me, and I think you know why). Dad then went on like that, marrying different teachers, being nice to them, and then cutting their heads off. When he got to Anne of Cleves, who Henry married but sent back for being too ugly, he chose this male teacher. That was BEYOND HILARIOUS because the teacher was really funny. He screwed his face right up and tried to give Dad a kiss. Dad looked horrified, the teacher then pretending to burst into tears when Dad sent him away. People were literally crying with laughter and I didn't think it could get any better.

But it did.

I already knew that Henry VIII's last wife was called Catherine Parr. She survived him – and guess who Dad chose to be her. Pretending to be really old now, and bloated, he staggered down from the stage and squinted round the audience. The kids were all screaming and pointing to their own teachers. I could tell that some of the teachers actually wanted to be chosen, but Dad didn't point to any of them. He pointed to Mum. She shrank back like the first teacher had, but I pushed her, and Dad then pulled her on to the stage. There he declared his undying love for her, and told her that he'd changed. He was no longer fickle. No longer selfish. He told her that he'd be true to her and that he'd never let her go. She was his heart's desire. And he sang 'Greensleeves' again, only this time he did it quietly, the whole room going silent. He sang it like he really meant it, and I thought Mum would laugh. Instead, however, she just looked into Dad's face, her mouth open as she moved her head very slowly from side to side. Everyone in the whole room was staring at them, and, when Dad finished, Mum went SO red. The whole crowd went, 'Ahhhhh!' and I did too because it was SO good to see them like that.

But then something caught my eye. The door to the next room was being opened.

Dad stood up and began to bow. Everyone around me started to cheer, but I moved off to the side, remembering why I'd wanted to come to Hall Place, and Hall Place alone (in the first place).

The teachers were collecting their classes together. I took Not Mr Fluffy back from one of them and pulled out my picture. Then I walked into the travelling exhibition. The first case held coins. I moved past. The second case held Elizabeth's piano keys and I thought of Veronique staring at them in wonder. I moved past those too because it was the third case that I wanted. I hurried towards it and squinted through the glass, just to check that the medal was still there. I was about to turn back and ask Mum. I wanted her to come through and take a picture of the medal because that would PROVE to Veronique that I'd been right. It would show that the medal in the case WAS a forgery. It had to be because, unlike the one I'd seen on the Internet, it had EIGHT white roses but only SIX red ones, instead of an equal amount.

Only . . .

I stopped.

And I counted.

And counted AGAIN.

And saw that the medal in the case did NOT have eight white roses and six red ones.

Not any more.

Now it had seven of each.

CHAPTER THIRTY-TWO

Jessica

I was still for a moment. And cold. Not just because of the fridge being open. All I could do was stare at the Fox & Sons brochure until I took a step back and looked round the kitchen, sensing the rooms beyond it and the garden, Boffo at the bottom. Our house.

We couldn't afford it. We only had one wage, and a nurse's wage at that. Everyone clapped for Mum and the people she works with during coronavirus, but she didn't get any more money afterwards.

So, what with Dad being ill, we couldn't afford to keep our house any more.

I couldn't believe it.

I wanted to get the house and wrap it up, hold it in my arms and not let go. I'm not saying it's particularly great. After we'd been to the Build-A-Bear Workshop for Anisa's birthday, we went back to her house and it was massive. She's got her own room and there's even this little playhouse in the garden. It's amazing but, however wonderful it is, it just isn't *our* house. Mum and Dad sometimes point to other houses when we're driving around – ones they nearly bought. I turn away because I don't like thinking that we might have lived somewhere else. The house wouldn't just have been different: we would have too. Our house doesn't just surround us and keep us warm (though we are SO lucky that it does). It lets us be us. And the fact that Mum was thinking of selling it made it feel like it was actually a house made out of cards. And it was all about to collapse.

Though I had no time to think about it.

To begin with I thought the noise was Mum – that she'd found out that I wasn't in bed. I panicked, but then I shook my head, preparing for her to come in. SHE wasn't going to tell ME off. How dare she do this, especially without talking to me? Hadn't we had that conversation at the hospital? Hadn't she confided in me? I stood up straight and got ready to confront her when she came downstairs into the kitchen.

But it wasn't Mum.

When no one called my name, I moved over to the kitchen door and saw something: the French windows, which lead out into the garden, were open. Dad never forgets to lock up and I frowned, trying to think of an explanation. Then I saw it: a dark figure fiddling with the shelves above our printer. I watched as it turned and walked out through the other door of the lounge into the hallway.

Was it Mum? Or Dad?

I didn't know and I nearly called out, but something told me not to. Instead, I just watched as the figure drifted past me to the stairs. Then it went up them, really slowly, hardly making a sound. At the top it stopped and looked around, a dot of light suddenly landing on Mum and Dad's door. When Milly and I were little, we did a picture of the two of them and, when the dot landed on that, it moved on, first to the bathroom door and then to our room, which has a pirate flag on, beneath which is a big sign I wrote which says,

!Keep Out!

But the figure took no notice of the sign – because a hand reached out and, VERY slowly, pushed the door open. Then it disappeared inside.

Our house is small, like I've said, but there's carpet on the stairs so I got up them without making a sound, then snuck a look round our bedroom door. For a second I thought that the figure had vanished, but then I saw it looking under my bed! The spot of light was going left and right before the figure moved over to Milly. All I could make out of my sister was a dark lump, but she must have been totally zonked out because she didn't move. The figure sent the dot of light under her bed and then straightened up.

As quickly as I could, I pulled my head back from the door, trying not to breathe. I knew I had to look again, though, so I did, with my fingers crossed. The figure was upright now, the yellow light flitting over our bookshelves before flicking first to Milly's bed and then to mine, where it lingered at the bottom, settling on all the different shapes there, stopping on one before lifting off again. Then it moved to the curtains, after which it bounced across my bedside table. It moved over my chest of drawers, dropping inside each one as, almost silently, the figure pulled each drawer open. And then it made its way round to me.

But it didn't get that far.

Instead, it hesitated, quivered and then stopped, and, when I saw where the light was, my heart seemed to jump like it wanted to leap RIGHT out of my chest.

CHAPTER THIRTY-THREE

Jessica

Our doll's house.

CHAPTER THIRTY-FOUR

Jessica

I grabbed hold of the door handle.

I took a deep breath.

I took an even deeper breath. And then I

SCREAMED.

CHAPTER THIRTY-FIVE

Cymbeline

Was I going mad? I counted again. And again. But each time there was an EQUAL number of roses. But that WASN'T what had been there before, something I knew because I'd counted loads of times, and drawn a picture afterwards! I shook my head, about to count AGAIN, when the helper came over – the same one as before.

'Can I help you?' she asked, once more staring at me through her big red glasses, her face, again, quite familiar. Perhaps it was only because of her make-up, though. She turned to Mum, who had followed me. 'Oh. It's . . . YOU.'

'Sorry?' Mum smiled. 'Have we . . . met?'

'What?' The helper was really staring at Mum. 'No,

I . . . It's your son.' She looked down at me again. 'You were here before, weren't you?'

'Yes, and . . .'

'Admiring the beautiful Phoenix Medal. Stunning, isn't it?'

'Yes, though the roses!'

'The what?'

'The number of roses!'

'Ah, I remember. You had an issue with that before, didn't you? I thought I'd explained it. But look . . .' The helper turned towards Dad, who was just walking in. 'Our wonderful Henry the Eighth. What a great show. You must come back and do it again. Really.'

'Wow,' said Dad. 'Thanks. I'd . . . love to.'

He scrabbled around in his pocket until he'd found his wallet, from which he produced a little card. He borrowed a pen from the helper and scribbled our address down.

'It's where I'm staying now.'

'Great,' the helper said, and grinned. I tried to get her attention again, but she ignored me and went off towards all the kids who were pouring in.

Dad asked what I thought of his performance. I said it was great, but I had something to tell him.

Something REALLY important! I pointed at the medal, but Dad interrupted. He said he'd sorted out a lift back to Lewisham with one of the schools and they were leaving now. Mum said, 'Great,' and she took my hand, pulling me out to where the coaches were waiting. I tried to tell her about the medal, but she didn't listen either, just calling out to Dad, to ask what coach it was. Then she called him outrageous again, though she *was* laughing now. She laughed some more when he did his Henry VIII voice to the kids climbing on to the coach. He did Henry VIII all the way back in fact, the whole coach laughing, Mum's eyes glued to him when I tried to talk to her. I was so cross. Yes, Mum and Dad were getting on, but something WEIRD had happened! Couldn't she see that?

Mum frowned. 'Cym,' she said. 'I really don't understand you. You asked to go to Hall Place with Dad and now you're all grumpy. Have you drunk enough water today?'

I said it wasn't ABOUT drinking water! Again I tried to explain – but Mum said I must have been mistaken. Then I couldn't say anything. The coach stopped to let us off near our school and we went inside so that Mum could vote. She got her ballot card and Dad and I watched her, standing at one of the booths they'd put up in the hall. As she was trying to decide who to vote for, she was humming 'Greensleeves' to herself, though I don't think she was really aware of it.

On the way home I thought about the helper. Had she deliberately ignored me just now? I didn't know, and Mum and Dad were too busy chatting to talk to about it. Soon we were home, and I had something else to think about: Not Mr Fluffy. I had to hide him before Ellen and Mabel got back. I did, but Ellen didn't stay home for long. She just packed a bag, and then Stephan took her round to Veronique's for their SLEEPOVER. I didn't know whether to be relieved or annoyed, though when Mabel came in that decision was easy. Stephan had left her with us and she charged at me while I was drinking a glass of milk. It went all over me.

'Is there any more?' I asked Mum, after I'd got changed. But the answer to that was no.

Mabel then made me play hide-and-seek with her, though she got bored while she was looking for me. She went off to do something else WITHOUT TELLING ME. I was in the washing basket for AGES.

When I finally realised, Mabel made me sit through THREE WHOLE EPISODES of *In the Night Garden*. That is one odd programme. It's like the sort of dream you might have if someone hit you over the head with a brick.

'Isn't it BRILLIANT, Thimbeline?'

'It's incredible.'

'Who do you like best? Iggle Piggle or the Tombliboos?'

'That's a very hard call to make.'

'I know! Choosing's hard. It would be like saying who's best between my daddy and your daddy, wouldn't it?'

I said I didn't know, and then braced myself for another episode.

I got lucky, though. Mabel said she was going upstairs to do some drawing and for some reason she decided not to make me go with her. Before she could change her mind, I snuck out into the garden (even though it was dark). I thought I could finally think about the Phoenix Medal, and I did. I wasn't going crazy. It had changed! I knew it had, and the fact that neither Mum nor Dad was interested made me so frustrated. Then I got even more frustrated because

Stephan came out and told me that he wanted a 'little chat'.

I g-r-o-a-n-e-d. Stephan had just got back from dropping Ellen off and now, like Mum, he was going to talk about how 'hard' it was for his girls. He was going to ask me to be 'patient' with Mabel. Worse, he was going to ask me to be 'understanding' of Ellen. I shook my head, wondering why adults always try to shift the way you think about things – to their point of view. Even when their point of view is WRONG. Why couldn't Stephan admit that his moving in COULDN'T WORK? Not even with a loft conversion. A million new bedrooms wouldn't make me as happy as before – the way it USED to be. So why didn't he see that, give up and take Mabel and Ellen with him?

And I was going to tell him that.

But Stephan's 'chat' was about something else.

And it was MUCH more interesting.

CHAPTER THIRTY-SIX

Cymbeline

'Cym,' Stephan said, after shutting the kitchen door behind him, 'I've been thinking about this break-in.'

'Oh?'

I was still suspicious of Stephan and I just watched him as he went over to the side of our shed. He pulled a ladder out.

'Yes,' he said. It was an extendable ladder and I watched him make it longer. 'They smashed the door down, right? The burglars?'

I nodded but I had to think about it. I'd been concentrating on the Phoenix Medal and the burglary seemed ages ago.

'That must have been noisy, though,' Stephan said.

'I suppose.'

'It must! Smashing a door in would make a right racket, and we know that Mr Fells doesn't miss much. He was here, wasn't he?'

'Yes.'

'Not off visiting his sister?'

'No.'

'So why didn't he come to investigate?'

'But he did,' I said.

'Yes, but only after you'd got home, right? The burglars made such a mess they must have been inside for a while.'

'So?'

'Why didn't he come before? Or, if not him, anyone?'

'Oh,' I said. 'I don't know.'

'Neither do I. So maybe the burglars *didn't* smash down the door to get in. Maybe they only did that at the end. Look.'

Stephan moved the ladder over to the back wall. Then he pointed to the fig tree. He'd cut some of the broken branches off and tied the others up with string. I scowled.

'Mum thinks I did that.'

'Well, I don't think you did.'

I blinked at him. 'Don't you?'

'No. You probably think it was Ellen, right?' Feeling a bit guilty, I nodded. 'Well, you're both too small. Go on, climb up.'

'What?'

'Use the branches that aren't broken. Go on.'

'I can't. Mum says I'm not allowed on the roof.'

'Then we'd better not tell her, had we?'

I looked at Stephan and shrugged. If he was willing to take the blame . . . I got up the tree in seconds and then I was looking down at him. 'See?' he said. 'You're far too light to harm it! And so is Ellen. Budge up.'

I did that and Stephan climbed up the ladder. He stood beside me on the flat grey roof, before walking over to the far edge, away from our garden. He knelt down and peered over.

'Look,' he said.

I walked over and knelt beside him, putting my hands out so I didn't fall off. And I saw what Stephan was pointing to. There was a drainpipe going down the far side of the garage to the ground – and part of it had been pulled off the wall.

'So did they climb up that?' I said. 'From behind the garages?'

'Who knows? Looks like it, though. If they did, they then went down the fig tree, which they broke.'

'But how did they get in the house?'

'Easy. Through the bathroom window. Your mum tends to leave it open, doesn't she?'

'It *was* open!'

'I know. And look, that gutter's loose too.'

Stephan pointed to the top of the drainpipe and I nodded to myself. It sounded really plausible. But I frowned. 'How did you know this?' I asked.

'Ah.' Stephan smiled. 'I saw it earlier.'

'How?'

'I was up here.'

'Were you? On the garage roof?! Why?'

'I had an idea.'

'About what? What?'

But Stephan didn't answer. Instead, he moved past me and made his way back down the ladder into our garden again.

I followed him, puzzled. There was no point asking him again, though – he just strode over to the side of the shed where a big rectangle of thin wood was propped up that I hadn't noticed before.

'It's ply,' he said. 'Got it earlier.'

'For putting over the bathroom window?'

Stephan shook his head – but he still didn't explain. Instead, he opened the shed door and pulled his workbench out. He put the plywood on it while I thought of Dad calling Stephan Bob the Builder, and laughing about what Stephan did 'On the Bus'. He didn't reach for a hammer, though, instead pulling out an electric saw. I got ready to watch, but Stephan had a surprise: he handed me some plastic goggles.

'Got those for you earlier. And these.' He followed the goggles with a pair of thick, colourful gloves. 'Didn't think you'd want to use Ellen's.'

'But what are they for?'

Stephan pointed at a line on the plywood. 'You need to cut along that.'

I blinked at him. 'I do? With that?'

'Sure. Put those on,' he said.

I did. The goggles needed tightening and the gloves were really stiff. It was hard to move my fingers, especially when Stephan handed ME the saw.

'I feel like an astronaut,' I said. 'You know, on a spacewalk.'

Stephan laughed. 'That's a good description. I'll help get you started.'

And he did. He held my arms and together we set the blade down on the straight line. He told me to press the button near my finger and when I did I GASPED. The saw was SO loud. It was really jerky too and I immediately let go of the button. I didn't think I could actually do it, but Stephan looked at me.

'Ellen found it hard to use at first too.'

'What? Ellen's used this saw?'

'Sure. Lots of times now. With me of course. I was hoping she'd help us with this, but she's at Veronique's, isn't she? Want to try again?'

Did I? If Ellen could do it . . . I waited until Stephan was holding my arms and pressed the button again, vibrations sprinting up to my shoulder like mad ants. It felt fantastic, though, thrilling and dangerous but safe at the same time. Then it got even better – I pushed the blade forward and it worked! It cut right through the wood, going straight along the line as Stephan guided me. Then I realised that, while he was still right there, he'd actually let go. It was JUST ME holding the saw! I nearly panicked, but instead I concentrated SO hard, really hoping that Mum and Dad were watching from inside. When I stopped for a rest, I glanced in through the kitchen window, sure that they must have heard the noise. Mum was cooking, though, with her back to me, Dad sitting at the kitchen table, drinking wine as he chatted to her.

It was disappointing – but I had to focus. I turned the saw on again and pushed the blade forward until the end of the line came into view. And then, with the most satisfying *clonk*, the thinner bit of wood fell down on to the patio.

'Brilliant!' Stephan exclaimed, as I lifted my finger off the trigger and the sound of the saw died away. 'Think we've got a natural here. Let's do the other side, shall we?'

I glanced back through the window, but Mum and Dad still weren't paying attention.

So I did the other side, after which I asked Stephan what exactly we were making.

'Wait and see,' he said, and showed me how to use a normal handsaw. With it we cut some different, thicker wood. After that, he did get a hammer out, but it was me who used it, not him. I nailed the big bit of wood to one end of the plywood. It made a shallow ramp, which I stared at, still unable to work out what it was that we'd created. An art bench for Mum? Some sort of marble-run for Mabel? I had no idea – until Stephan told me to go up on to the garage roof again.

I climbed up the ladder this time and Stephan handed the ramp to me. He told me to set it down with the shallow end facing the garden, and I did, though still without a clue what it was for – until I'd climbed back down into the garden. Stephan tossed me my football.

'Go on,' he said. 'Kick it up.'

'On the roof? Really?'

'You'll see.'

And so I did, though first I put the ball down on the ground. I did this trick Billy Lee showed me: I moved my feet together really fast, which sent the ball up in front of me. Then I booted it, the ball arching up on to the roof, though it didn't stay there for long. Nothing happened for a second, but then I heard a rolling sound and the ball came shooting off, thumping down on the grass right beside me.

'That's brilliant!' I said. 'I won't have to climb up. It's brilliant!'

And it was. I kicked the ball up again, and again the ramp sent it down, on the other side of me this time. Stephan had a go and then we took turns, kicking it up and trying to catch it. That got too easy so we threw a tennis ball instead. I made Stephan use one hand, and start with his back to the wall, after which he had to spin round. Soon we were laughing like crazy and I SO wanted to show this to Lance. And Veronique! She's not interested in football, but she'd LOVE this. She does fencing after school and she'd be great at it.

Stephan said that I had to start with my back to the wall too, but I still won (10–9 after Stephan dropped the last one). I squealed out, 'YES!' and did a lap of honour round the garden as Stephan shouted, 'Boo!' After that, I pretended I was on an open-top bus going round London with the winner's trophy. Stephan shook his head.

'Thanks,' I said, when I'd tormented him enough. 'It's great. We've had that problem with the ball forever. I can't believe we didn't think of it. Though . . .' I stared up at the roof as Stephan walked over to his workbench. He put it away and went back for the ladder, which was still leaning near the fig tree.

'Yes?'

'Well. If the burglars climbed over the garage and in through the bathroom window, why did they smash the door in at the *end*? It doesn't make sense.'

'I know,' Stephan said. 'Not if it was a normal burglary. They would have left the same way they came in. But what if they only wanted to make it *look* like a burglary?'

'So it wasn't one?'

'I don't think so.'

'Then what was it?'

Stephan turned and stared at the house, where Dad must have told Mum another joke because she was laughing again. 'I think they were looking for something.'

CHAPTER THIRTY-SEVEN

Cymbeline

'Looking for something?' I asked. It's what I'd said to Veronique, and I remembered our conversation. 'They can't have been.'

'Why not?' Stephan frowned.

'Because my bedroom was the one they trashed the most,' I explained. 'They hardly touched Mum's. What could they have wanted from MY room?'

'Who knows?' Stephan put my gloves and goggles away and shut the shed door. 'What did they take?'

'From me? Nothing.'

'And from the rest of the house?'

'Mum's iPad. And a Bluetooth speaker. And some painting of hers.'

'So I'd think about those things, yes?'

I said I would but I wasn't convinced he was right – until I remembered something. Veronique's mum had said that, in *their* burglary, Auntie Mill's CCTV didn't show the burglars going in. So maybe they got in the back of their house too, and then broke the door afterwards. And, if that was the case, then it HAD to be the same burglars – but it also meant something else. If they were looking for something, and they THEN went to Veronique's house, they couldn't have found it at mine, could they?

But did they find it at hers?

I wanted to ask Veronique right way. I was about to go in and get Mum to call her, and on another day I would have. But I had an image of her and Ellen – p-l-a-y-i-n-g together. They'd be doing each other's hair, or admiring their stupid friendship bracelets. Veronique wouldn't even listen to me; she'd say I was 'so funny sometimes'. I seethed inside and just waited for Stephan to finish packing up. Then I told him about Hall Place.

'Wow,' he said, not trying to dismiss me like Mum had. 'You're sure that the medal had a different number of roses before? And that they're equal now?'

'Yes!'

'Well, that *is* strange. Let me think about it. And I know someone who loves puzzles like this. Solving things. I'll talk to them . . . if that's all right?'

'It's great,' I said, and I nodded, SO relieved that someone had taken me seriously. But then I had another thought. The medal and the burglary: they'd happened at roughly the same time, hadn't they? So were they connected to each other?

I couldn't think how, so I shook my head and ran inside.

I told Mum about the ramp. She said it sounded fantastic, but she was still cooking and I could tell she wasn't paying attention. She didn't ask to come outside for me to show her and neither did Dad. He was on his phone. When Stephan came in, I thought Mum would thank him for making it, but she just gave him this forced sort of smile as he washed his hands in the sink. Then Mabel ran through and bashed into Mum's leg – and Mum snapped at her! This is something I'd been hoping for for DAYS, desperate for Mum to treat her and Ellen normally AND TELL THEM OFF. But, actually, I wished Mum hadn't snapped at Mabel then. She was just excited because she'd finished her picture – which turned out to be for me.

And I have to admit that it was great.

Mabel had drawn a football match. But not a normal one. She'd drawn a unicorn football match, little unicorns all surrounding this big unicorn, who was about to score a goal. The unicorn had a red shirt on (Charlton) and my name on the side.

Spelled FIMBALEEN.

That was even further away from reality than Mabel normally got, but she was so proud of the picture. I thought Mum's snapping might make her cry so, very quickly, I took her upstairs. I got some Blu-tack from my art box and put the picture up on my door. This did cheer her up, but not completely. Mabel looked serious. Very serious. She stared up at me with her massive brown eyes, and then she asked me something that made me feel

TERRIBLE.

'Thimbeline,' she said, her voice all trembly. 'Are you glad that we came to live in your house with you?'

I blinked. The question was like a missile blowing up everything inside me. 'Why are you asking?' I croaked.

'It's Daddy,' Mabel said.

'What about him?'

'Well, he said something really weird. To Ellen and me. He told us that it's *hard* for you. Us being here. IS it hard for you, Thimbeline?'

'Well . . .'

'He told us. He said it's a big change. He said we have to be really nice to you, which is why I made you that picture.' She pointed to the red unicorn. 'A Charlton-corn. To make you feel better. Does it?'

'Does it?'

'Make you feel better?'

And I opened my mouth to reply, seeing the picture properly for the first time. The team the red unicorn was playing against all had twisted horns and downturned faces. They were clearly meant to be evil, but only then did I realise that they were all blue – which could mean only one thing.

They were Millwall unicorns.

Mill-corns.

That Mabel had drawn me triumphing over evil Millwall unicorns was SO nice of her. I also thought about Stephan and the ramp – but THEN I thought about Ellen again. She'd stolen my biscuits! She'd booted me in the face! She'd stolen Not Mr Fluffy AND she'd stolen my friend. I wasn't going to lie – I still wished that they would GO.

'It . . .'

'Yes, Thimbeline?'

But Mum called me to come down, so I didn't have to answer. And she had something to tell me.

I thought it must be suppertime – but Stephan wasn't in the kitchen and neither was Dad. Instead, sitting at the table was someone who made me stop in my tracks: Veronique's mum! I hadn't heard her come in and I stared, this sharp, glinting thrill inside me. Was it Ellen? Had she done something terrible?! Had Veronique's mum brought her home in disgrace? The glee ripped through me as I looked around – but she wasn't there, which was when I realised that Mrs Chang didn't seem angry. She looked a little worried, and so did Mum.

'What is it?' I said. Mum put her teacup down on the table and so did Mrs Chang. 'Has something happened?'

'No,' Mum said. 'Nothing new. Just something we need to ask you.'

'Oh?'

'Yes,' said Veronique's mum. 'It's a bit odd. About your burglary.'

'The door?'

'No. Not that.'

'Is it Veronique's room? Was it messed up more than anywhere else?'

Veronique's mum looked surprised. 'Yes. How did you . . . ?'

'Mine was too, though nothing's missing. Was anything taken from Veronique's room?'

'No,' said her mum. 'That's the thing, though something happened. Veronique didn't tell me about it at the time because it upset her, and you know that she struggles with her feelings, don't you? Understanding them?'

I did. And I also knew that she struggled with understanding the feelings of her best friend! 'So what happened?'

'Your teddies,' Mum said.

'What about them?'

'None of them are missing?'

I'd checked that when I'd had to lend one to Mabel. 'No.'

'And nothing else is wrong with them?'

'Wrong with them?'

'Yes,' Veronique's mum said. 'Like Veronique's teddies.'

'Not Cyrano de Bergerac!' He was Veronique's **!Teddy of Most Extreme Importance!**, a yellow elephant she'd got in France.

'No. He was fine. But some of the others . . .'

'Yes?'

'Were attacked. With scissors or a knife. It really upset Veronique and I just wondered if any of yours were like that.'

'Mine?' I said.

And I ran upstairs. I brought my teddy basket down – two dinosaurs, three snakes, a crocodile, a horse from Pippy Longstocking, a panda, Uncle Bulgaria (Womble), this Olympic one whose name I've forgotten and Paddington. They were all fine. Tiny Clanger was too, and Not Mr Fluffy (though he wasn't there at the time).

'Why did they do it?' I said.

'Just nasty, I guess. And bizarre.'

'Bizarre?'

'Well, they didn't do the ones that were animals, or characters. They just damaged the ones that looked normal.'

'The teddy teddies?'

'That's right. Anyway, I'm glad it didn't happen to you. I just wanted to come and check.'

'Is Veronique okay?' Veronique's mum looked a bit shifty.

'She is now. She's . . .'

I sighed. 'Having fun with Ellen?'

'Yes. They're . . . getting on very well.'

'*Great*. I'm very glad to hear it,' I said, and I was about to turn away and go back upstairs, but Dad came in.

'You'll never guess what?!' he exclaimed.

'Go on,' Mum said.

'Hall Place.'

'What about it?'

'They want me to do more workshops. Probably a regular thing.'

'That's good.'

'Good? It's great! Having something so close to home like that.'

'Home?' I said.

'It's fantastic!' Dad went on.

'So is it definite then?'

'Think so. She loved it, particularly the baby thing.

Great idea, that. Anyway, she wants to meet up to discuss it.'

'Who does?'

'The woman – who we spoke to at the end? The helper Cym met when he was there before. She's in charge of events. She wants to talk about it and she also said sorry for not having time to chat before. So she wants Cym to be there too.

'Cool, huh?'

CHAPTER THIRTY-EIGHT

Jessica

They didn't believe us.

Not Mum, or Dad, OR the police. *They* got there about ten minutes after I screamed. The figure was gone by then. It had spun round, the torchlight blinding me so that I couldn't see its face. It lurched past me and ran down the stairs. I hurried back into our bedroom and flung the curtains open. Milly bolted upright and asked what was wrong, but I didn't answer, just staring down into the garden until the figure came out of the French windows. It galloped down our garden, leapt on to Boffo's hutch and climbed the back fence.

And the bedroom light came on.

'Jess!' Mum shrieked. 'What is it?'

I told her. And, when the police came, I told them.

There were lots of police people. Four came in the house (Mum had turned ALL the lights on) and some more went into the garden, looking at the fence, then seeing if they could get any shoe prints from the flowerbeds (so Dad said). They were brilliant, actually, and so was Mum – until I told them about Mr Goldy.

'What?' Mum said. We were sitting at the kitchen table: Mum, Dad, Milly, me and two police officers. 'That one you found at Cuckmere?'

'*Yes*,' I said.

'But you gave that back to the woman who came round.'

I sighed and told her that we hadn't, and then had to start from the beginning because the police officers were confused.

'Look,' I said, 'it's simple. We found a teddy and we argued about it. Mum put a photo on WhatsApp so that its owner could come and get it.'

The older police officer nodded to the younger one, who was taking notes.

'Then this woman came round to pick the teddy up. Only –' I glanced at Milly – 'we gave her a different one. She took it away, but then she cut it open and left it in a bin.'

'She . . . cut it open? A teddy bear?'

'Yes! But it was the *wrong* teddy.'

'The wrong . . . ?'

'Teddy! And now she's come back for the right one.'

The older police officer scratched the back of his head. The younger one waited with her pencil ready. 'The *right* teddy?'

'Yes! That's what she was looking for!'

'And you know this because . . . ?'

'She went straight to our room and searched for it.'

'Well.' The older police officer shrugged. 'We'd better see this teddy bear, hadn't we? If it's of such immense importance to the burgling community.'

I ran upstairs.

'Here,' I said thirty seconds later. I'd pulled Mr Goldy out of the doll's house, and I set him down on the table.

'Well, that *is* a very nice-looking teddy bear. He's very . . .'

The younger police officer looked up from her notebook. 'Yes, Sarge?'

'Cute. Cuddly, you could say. What do you think, Constable?'

'Oh yes, Sarge. *Very* cuddly, though that's not a particularly accurate description.'

'No,' the first police officer agreed. 'I suppose that a lot of teddies could be described as "cuddly". That is, of course, the intention of the manufacturers. So what we have here is a classic-style English teddy bear, approximately thirty-five centimetres in height, without any ribbons or other identifiable clothing. Legs, chubby. Tummy, round. Eyes, brown. Fur, also brown.'

'I'd say gold, Sarge.'

'Correction. Colour of fur, gold. It is also extremely . . .' He hesitated.

'Yes, Sarge?'

'Downy. Would you say downy, Constable?

'No, Sarge, I wouldn't say downy. I think I would say . . .'

'Yes, Constable?'

'Velvety.'

'Velvety?! Oh no! Look at it for goodness' sake!'

'Sorry, Sarge. Silky then?'

'NO! It's not silky either. It's. Well, it's . . .' The older police officer sighed in frustration. But then he sat up.

'FLUFFY!' he said, and he turned to the constable

who gave him a high-five. She wrote FLUFFY on her pad in big letters – but neither of them would believe that someone had broken into our house to steal it!

And neither would Mum or Dad.

'It's not old enough to be rare,' Dad said. 'It's not an antique. We know you both love it, but still . . .'

And all four of them looked at me with this patient ADULT expression that made me want to SCREAM. Instead of doing that, though, I hissed and pulled Mr Goldy to my chest. Then I described the intruder.

I told the police officers all I could. I said the figure was tall. It wasn't slim but not necessarily fat or anything – just like the lady who'd come round! Mrs Rose! I described her short grey curly hair and her red glasses. I could tell that the police officers didn't think it was the same person, though. They just thanked me and went outside, Mum asking if I wanted a hot chocolate. I shrugged, still SO frustrated. Mum took that to mean yes, though, and went over to the worktop – where the Fox & Sons brochure was sitting next to the kettle.

Mum gave a little jerk. She slid the brochure into a drawer, not knowing that I'd already seen it. My frustration turned back to anger. I felt hot and helpless, wanting to just storm over there and pull the brochure out. Demand to know what Mum was playing at. The fact that I didn't was because Milly was there – and then because of something else.

The most OBVIOUS thing had occurred to me. I wasn't the only one who loved our house, was I? It was Mum's house too.

So how must she feel about it?

The anger seemed to drift right out of me. When Mum put the hot chocolate down, I didn't scowl. Instead, I smiled and took her hand. I held it and glanced at the drawer, Mum giving a small gasp, before pulling me into a hug. It was so brilliant I wanted to stay in it forever, but it wasn't long before she drew away. Then I watched her help Dad back up the stairs, knowing that, after she came back, she'd have to deal with us. And, a few hours later, she'd be back at work.

How on earth did she do it?

I didn't know, though the next day she actually didn't go to work. Dad wasn't well enough. Mum said it was the medicine he was on. It didn't agree with him. The day after she did go, but had to come back halfway through. It was like that all week and so hard on

301

Mum, even though Milly and I did all we could. We cleaned out Boffo. We put the washing in the machine. We hung it up after. We got our clothes out for the morning and made our own packed lunches. Milly missed after-school rugby to do the ironing and I didn't go to art club. I cleaned the bathroom instead. Milly got really good at making cups of tea and I did us cheesy beans in the microwave (two minutes four seconds EXACTLY).

And things seemed to go okay.

Dad's new medicine was better. He didn't feel so groggy, or sick.

Then – Tuesday – he got a letter. It said he had to go to London at the weekend for some special tests. There was this new treatment that he might be eligible for. It made him happy and he got even happier when he realised that Brighton were playing some London team in the FA Cup. Milly and I don't care about football, but we begged to go too.

'We'll see,' Dad said, which SO meant yes. We still had Mr Goldy and the intruder to think about, though. Not only did Mum have to pay for better locks on the French windows, but the police hadn't caught anyone.

'It was her!' I said. We'd just tidied our room. 'I promise.'

Milly said she believed me.

'And I've been thinking. If Mr Goldy really was hers, why didn't she come back? When she realised that we'd tricked her?'

Milly nodded. 'She must have thought we wouldn't hand him over so she decided to steal him instead.'

'So how can we know if she was lying or not, about whether Mr Goldy *was* hers?'

Milly sighed. 'Rivers.'

'What about them?'

'We did them in school before Christmas. They come from places.'

'Of course they do! So?'

'So we should have asked Mrs Rose where her grandson dropped Mr Goldy in.'

'She said son to Mum.'

'I know. It's so fishy! But her telling us where Mr Goldy went in the river would have told us if he really could have floated to Cuckmere Haven.'

'But I did ask her!' I insisted. 'She started to answer but she stopped herself. She said I wouldn't know it.'

303

'Come on,' said Milly, and she pulled me down the stairs.

We got the laptop and opened it on the kitchen table. We went into Maps and found Cuckmere Haven. The caption said that it was a 'tranquil beach with cliff views'.

'It wasn't tranquil when we were there.'

'No,' I laughed. 'It wasn't.'

We traced the river back inland. It was called the Cuckmere River, and first it went up through a forest. It ran alongside a pub called the Plough and Harrow, though that wasn't what Mrs Rose had nearly said. I was sure! The river passed a big lake, before flowing through the moat of a castle. People do visit castles and I was excited: but, again, the name wasn't right. I shook my head and we scrolled up some more, the river spreading out now like the branches of a blue tree, any one of which would have brought Mr Goldy down to Cuckmere! It was frustrating, though not many of the little rivers had actual places on. But one did – and my finger darted to the screen.

'Whitecross House,' I said.

Milly's eyes spun round to me. 'Did she say that?'

I shrugged, thinking maybe, so Milly clicked on the

link. On the left of the screen lots of information appeared, all about Whitecross House. There was another link for its own website and Milly clicked on it. Pictures came up of a big house, the inside full of four-poster beds and long, shiny dining tables. These scrolled past and were followed by photos of the outside. First there was a garden with tall hedges – and then there was a river bank! In the next one were lots of people having picnics! Some of them were kids and I could so imagine them messing about, perhaps playing Pooh Sticks like we had.

Did one of them drop Mr Goldy in the river? Right there? It was possible, but how could we know for certain?

'Is that where you came from?' I said, turning to Mr Goldy. He was on the kitchen table because we hardly let him out of our sight any more. But Mr Goldy didn't reply, which I thought was just a *little* ungrateful after all we'd done for him. I shrugged and Milly did too, before her finger reached out for the mouse pad again. She was about to close the page down, but I stopped her.

'Wait,' I said, pointing to the top of the screen.

I was looking at a line of headings. Milly moved

the cursor up to them. The first said 'Plan Your Visit' and I knew that, if Milly clicked on it, there would be subheadings underneath. Beside 'Plan Your Visit' was a heading called 'Events', and then two more: 'Kids' and 'Wedding Hire'. It was the last one that I wanted, though.

'Shop'.

'Click on it,' I said and Milly did.

And her mouth dropped **WIDE OPEN**.

'Gucci,' she said.

CHAPTER THIRTY-NINE

Jessica

There were tea towels for sale (one for £5.99 or two for £10.00).

There were teapots (two, four or six cups).

There were coffee mugs, there were pencil sets, there were powerballs and sticker books, none of which were of any interest to us at all.

Because of the teddies.

They weren't called teddies. They were called 'Soft Toys', which is SO wrong. TEDDIES AREN'T TOYS! They're something else, something deeper and more serious, which I can't quite explain. But there were loads of them.

There were small teddies.

And big ones.

There were fat teddies.

And thin ones.

There were colourful teddies and regular ones. There were Gruffalos and Paddingtons, Eeyores and Winnie the Poohs. They even had the Tiger Who Came to Tea, which normally I SO would have wanted.

But I was looking at Mr Goldy.

They didn't call him that (though he SO is Mr Goldy). They called him 'Whitecross Bear' – but it was him. Or at least a clone of him and, when I turned back to the table, it was spooky. It was probably just the light from the screen, but I could swear that Mr Goldy's eyes were twinkling.

'Found you!' said Milly, though I wasn't so happy. The river connected Whitecross House to Cuckmere Haven, which meant that Mr Goldy might really belong to Mrs Rose. What if she came back for him? What if she pretended she hadn't tried to burgle us and just turned up?

I gripped Mr Goldy tight and went to look out of the window. There was no one there, but I couldn't stop worrying, imagining that the doorbell was going to ring any second. I worried about it all day, even waking up in the night. The next day I worried about it at school and when I got back I thought my worst fears had come true.

Because Mum called us into the living room.

She looked drawn. Exhausted. Worst of all she looked SO miserable. The first thing she did was give us both a massive hug and I bit my lip, determined not to complain, not to make things any worse for her. Mr Goldy was in my schoolbag and I'd just have to go and get him.

But Mum didn't ask us for Mr Goldy.

She didn't tell us that Mrs Rose had been back in touch.

She didn't say anything in fact – she couldn't. When she tried, she just started to sob, and all we could do was look at her, with no idea what we should do, until there was a noise outside.

Was it Mrs Rose? Had she come back? I didn't care. I'd just hand Mr Goldy over so that she'd go away and I could go back in to be with Mum. I ran to the door and pulled it open, though it wasn't Mrs Rose that I saw.

It was a man. He was lifting something out of the back of his car. I blinked, confused, until I realised who it was.

I felt Milly behind me. Her fingernails dug into my arm and stayed there until the Fox & Sons man was gone.

CHAPTER FORTY

Cymbeline

The one good thing about Ellen being at Veronique's house was that she wasn't around on Saturday morning. I watched TV in peace until it was time to go up to Saturday football. I can go on my own, but I wanted Dad to take me. He was still in bed, though, so Mum said she'd come. She started to put her coat on, but Stephan stopped her. He said he fancied a walk, and then turned to Mabel (who was halfway through her rice crispies).

'You'd like to watch Cym play football, wouldn't you, love?'

Mabel looked REALLY excited and ran upstairs to clean her teeth.

Mum hung her coat back up and Stephan put his

on. I thought we might be late because Mabel had to stuff loads of things in her unicorn backpack. Stephan pulled her on a scooter, though, and we made good time, in spite of the fact that she kept leaping off to jump in puddles. Stephan explained that puddles were the only things that she liked as much as unicorns, so I got a stick and stuck it in one.

'It's a uni-puddle,' I said.

We made three more uni-puddles and then turned off the main road.

Stephan looked at me. 'Been thinking more about the burglary,' he said.

'Oh yes?'

Stephan nodded. 'I asked your mum about the painting that was stolen, but all she said was that it was a landscape. She didn't want to talk about it. She also didn't think there was anything special on the iPad. So then I thought about your room and that friend of yours. Veronique?'

Was she still my friend? 'And?'

'Does she have anything of yours?'

'What do you mean?'

'Well, that the burglars might have wanted, but didn't find in your bedroom?'

I shrugged. 'I don't think so.'

'Nothing you've left behind after a sleepover maybe?'

'No. And she said that nothing of hers was taken anyway.'

'Right. Well, I spoke to the police again. They're going to come back to fingerprint the gutters. You never know, they might find something.'

'Wow,' I said, amazed that Stephan had gone that far. 'What about the Phoenix Medal? What do you think about that then?'

Stephan sucked his cheeks in. 'I haven't managed to speak to the person I mentioned. The one who's good at puzzles. Ask me later, okay?'

I said okay and we walked on, spotting all the players up ahead, spread across the grass.

We were on time and I was glad: we had league matches next week and I wanted to be in the starting seven. Mabel was a worry, though: it would be SO embarrassing if she started shouting, 'Go, Thimbeline!' from the touchline. Marcus Breen would shred me. I was about to suggest that Stephan take her into Blackheath Village for a hot chocolate, but Mabel pointed to the Reception team, whose coach was just getting some cones out.

'*What?*' she screamed. 'Do little ones play football too, Thimbeline?'

I said they do, which was when Vi, Daisy and Lizzie Fisher came up. They'd all just started playing for Lewisham Girls and had their new tracksuits on. Normally I would have been jealous, but when they saw how excited Mabel was Vi passed a ball to her. Mabel hoofed it back and then ran at Vi to tackle her. Vi laughed and I told her who Mabel was.

'Do you want to join in?' Vi asked.

'*REALLY?*' Mabel said.

Vi said, 'Really!' and took Mabel over to the Reception team, staying to help coach them because one of the parents couldn't make it that day.

I was relieved, though after we'd done some warm-ups and a few passing drills I sighed. Veronique's dad was walking towards us. Veronique wasn't with him – she has piano lessons on Saturday mornings – but Ellen was. He was obviously dropping her off. Ellen said thank you to him and I bit my lip, noticing the FOUR friendship bracelets that were now circling her wrists.

I shook my head, knowing that she'd gloat, though she'd have to wait until I'd finished training. That thought made me nod and tell myself to concentrate. Stephan was staying to watch both Mabel and me, so Ellen would have to as well, and I didn't want to give her anything to laugh at. I wanted to play well, maybe even score, so at least I'd have that to tell her when she started droning on about Veronique.

Ellen and Stephan came over to the touchline just as we started to play. When the ball went off for a throw-in, I was quite close to them and I expected Ellen to say something. She didn't, though – she and Stephan were talking. The next time I saw her she was looking at Stephan's mobile phone, and when I glanced over again (free kick) she was still doing it. That was a REAL shame because I DID score, doing a one-two with Lance before nutmegging the goalkeeper (Daisy's dad, but he DID NOT LET ME DO IT). There was no way Ellen would believe me when I told her, though Stephan saw it. I knew that because he did this big fist pump, clapped and bellowed, 'GET IN!' at the top of his voice.

That made me blush – and feel odd. And – *weirdly* – a bit sad. I didn't know why, I just did, as if that really good thing – scoring a goal in front of Stephan – had uncovered something that wasn't good. I bit my lip and ran back to the halfway line, confused. I couldn't wait to tell Dad, though, and I wondered if he'd actually come up after all and seen it. But he hadn't.

I didn't mind, though, when Stephan went over to watch Mabel's match. I took a breath. Would Ellen take the opportunity to gloat about last night? I tried to anticipate what she'd say: did they watch a movie together? The second *Harry Potter* that Mum says I'm too young for? Did they arrange to have another play date at our house – without me being invited? Or was it Kit-Kat, the Lego rat that I'd made for Veronique? Had Ellen broken it up and made something else with the pieces, like Mabel had with the Death Star? I didn't know but I was about to find out. Vi's dad (our coach) blew his whistle for full time, and Ellen came marching over.

'I don't care,' I said.

Ellen stared at me. 'About what?'

I shrugged. 'About anything. That you did. So you can tell me if you like.'

'Tell you?'

'Yeah, go on. Smash it, did you?'

'*Smash what?*'

'Veronique's rat. That I made her? Did you?'

'No!'

'Probably didn't see it then.'

Ellen's eyes flared. 'Wrong. Veronique showed it to me.'

'Oh. She . . . did?'

'Yes, and I was *going* to say that it was really good. Don't think I'll bother now, *or* show you this.'

'This?'

'Yes,' Ellen said, and she held Stephan's mobile out to me.

I was curious, but then I shook my head. Was it a picture of her and Veronique, all smiley? Had Veronique's dad sent it to Stephan?

'No thanks. I'm not stupid.'

'No? You must be if you haven't thought to do this before.'

'Do what?'

Ellen hissed out a sigh. 'Try to find the Phoenix Medal of course.'

CHAPTER FORTY-ONE

Cymbeline

'*What?*' I said.

Ellen pushed her hair behind her ears. 'Dad just told me about it. He said you need help.'

I blinked at her. So it was ELLEN who Stephan meant! 'From YOU?'

'Yes, from me. He knows I like puzzles.'

'As much as you like Jaffa Cakes and chocolate fingers? And Not Mr Fluffy?'

'Who?'

'My . . . teddy! Not to mention stealing my friend, and getting Mabel to use all my Lego. Well?'

'I . . .'

'You what? Go on, tell me! Or deny it – say that you didn't do any of those things. Well?'

'Well . . .' Ellen swallowed.

'YES?'

'Well, I just found . . .' Ellen looked down at her shoes. From across the grass came another big cheer from Stephan. Mabel had scored a goal. 'I found it hard.'

'YOU did?' I laughed. 'Moving into MY house? What about me?'

'I know, Cymbeline.' Ellen winced. 'Dad said. But it's hard for me too.'

'*What?* How?'

'Moving here. It's made it all really final.'

'Made what final?'

'My mum. And . . .'

'Yes?'

'My dad.'

I hesitated. 'What . . . about them?'

'Well, yours split up when you were a baby, didn't they?'

I hesitated again, but nodded, not really sure where this was going. 'So?'

'So it won't have bothered you, will it?'

'I suppose not, but . . .'

'But mine only split up two years ago. It was

really hard. You can't believe how hard. And I kept thinking . . .'

'What?'

Ellen looked at her shoes. 'That they'd get back together.'

I didn't know what to say to that. 'Oh.'

'And I so wanted them to. I dreamed about it almost every night. I kept asking why they couldn't make up, just like Dad tells me and Mabel to when we argue. But they didn't make up, or not enough to stay with each other. And moving in with you means that they won't. Not ever.'

'Oh,' I said again. 'And you wanted to make it bad at our house so your dad would take you away again?'

'Yes,' Ellen whispered, and I stared at her.

'So what have you found then?'

'Found?'

I tapped Stephan's phone. 'On that.'

Ellen looked up at me. 'Oh. The medal – it was at Hall Place, right?'

'Yes,' I said.

'And it changed its roses?'

'It did. I am NOT making it up!'

'I know! Dad said. So I believe you. But the medal actually doesn't live there, does it?'

'No,' I admitted. 'It's part of a travelling exhibition. But what . . . ?'

'As I've just discovered. Did you never think to wonder where *else* it might have travelled to?'

No. I hadn't. 'But why should I?'

'Because there might be other reports of it being weird. Looking different. Yes?'

'Er . . . yes? So you've . . . ?'

'Got a list. It wasn't hard to find. Heard of Google? You should have told me about this earlier. Anyway, it's here – all the places the Phoenix Medal has *ever* been loaned to.'

'Right,' I said. 'So we can . . .'

'Phone them up. We can ask if anything happened when the medal was there. What do you think?'

What I thought was that it was a good idea. It might not work but it was something – and I hadn't been able to think of ANYTHING to do. So I stared at Stephan's phone, squinting at the list – all the places the medal had been. The first was somewhere called Anglesey Abbey. Then there was Boarstall Tower (they were in alphabetical order). After that came Dalton

321

Castle and Kingston Lacy, followed by Lodge Park, Old Soar Manor and Smallhythe Place, though it didn't say where any of these places were.

'Doesn't matter,' Ellen said. 'All we've got to do is phone them. There aren't that many.'

'No, wait,' I said. 'Scroll down a bit, will you?'

I said that because the list carried on, continuing beyond the bottom of the screen. There can't have been too many more because we were already up to S with Smallhythe Place, but I wanted to see them all. So Ellen did scroll down, swiping her finger up to the next name.

Sudbury Hall.

And the next.

Tattershall Castle.

And then she swiped again and the next name seemed to leap right off the phone and punch me in the face.

CHAPTER FORTY-TWO

Cymbeline

Whitecross House.

CHAPTER FORTY-THREE

Cymbeline

'Mum!'

Stephan had unlocked our front door and I'd shoved it open.

'Cym?' Mum said. 'What is it?'

I ran into the kitchen. 'The painting, Mum, that was stolen. Was it one of your . . . special ones?'

Mum's eyes widened in shock and I could tell she didn't want to answer. But she nodded.

'Of Whitecross House?'

She nodded again. 'It's okay, though. I have a couple more.'

At one time she'd had loads more, as it was all she ever painted – because of my twin brother Anthony dying. The painting showed the picnic rug that I'd been sitting on with Anthony, near the river. It showed Mr Fluffy, actually, but what was more important was that we'd been to Whitecross House again – six months ago. Mum had nearly drowned in the river.

'And the Phoenix Medal I saw at Hall Place was also at Whitecross House!'

Mum frowned at me. 'So?'

'Listen,' I said. 'The one at Hall Place IS a fake. They must have got the roses wrong and only realised when I spotted it. So they changed them to make it look right.'

'Okay, but . . . ?'

'But we've also been burgled, haven't we? And not just us. Veronique's been burgled too. And our bedrooms were the worst!'

'So?'

'So Veronique came with us to Whitecross House, didn't she? The second time?'

'Yes, but I still don't—'

'Get it? But it's obvious!'

'Is it?'

'Yes! Mum, the burglars must think that I've got it. Or that Veronique has!'

'Got what?'

'Mum! Pay attention. They must think that one of us has the REAL Phoenix Medal. That's what they came here looking for!'

'But how could you?' Mum said.

'How could I what?'

'Have the Phoenix Medal? The real one? How could you have it, Cym?'

I had no answer to that. Veronique and I didn't even go inside Whitecross House, or know that the Phoenix Medal was there. We'd stayed outside. It was confusing, but I knew what I had to do to find out. 'We've got to go to Hall Place!' I said. 'And speak to them. We've got to tell them what happened. And, Mum!'

'What is it, Cym?'

'I recognised her! The helper woman at Hall Place! I knew that I'd seen her before. Maybe it was at Whitecross House. Maybe that's where I first saw her!'

'Saw who?' Dad said, as he sauntered into the kitchen.

Dad had shaved. He'd also ironed his shirt and was wearing his best jeans.

'The woman from Hall Place,' I said. 'You know, who we spoke to at the end.'

'Well, that's funny,' Dad said.

'What is?'

'I've just been speaking to her.'

'*Speaking to her?*'

'About being Henry the Eighth. The woman from Hall Place. You remember that she wanted me to meet her to talk about it?'

'Yes?'

'Well, she wants to meet right now. And she still wants to see you too.'

'When?' I said.

'Right now.'

I stared at him. 'Me?'

'That's what she said. Probably because you were so into the house, you know? She said you were very interesting. Well, shall we go, then?' Dad said.

CHAPTER FORTY-FOUR

Cymbeline

'To Hall Place?' I asked, but Dad shook his head.

'She's down in Greenwich today. She works at the *Cutty Sark* too. She wants us to go and meet her there.'

The *Cutty Sark* is this huge former tea clipper, a sailing boat that went all round the world delivering things (before the Internet took over). It lives in Greenwich and is a bit of a landmark. People come from all over to see it.

'Much more convenient than Hall Place,' Dad went on. 'And maybe I can get some work on the *Cutty Sark* too. I said we'd see her in half an hour, okay?'

I said okay, though half an hour? That gave me almost no time to think. Would I say anything to her? About the Phoenix Medal? What if she just laughed at me? I had to find out more first, though I couldn't ask Dad for help. He was too focused on getting this new job. He wouldn't want anything to get in the way of that and he wasn't interested in my thoughts about the Phoenix Medal anyway. I was still trying to think of a plan when Ellen piped up.

'The *Cutty Sark*? That big ship you can see? Can we go too, Dad?'

Stephan shrugged, and so did Mum. So we bundled out of the door. It had just stopped raining, but Dad thought it might start again. He wanted to get a taxi.

'I need to compose myself,' he said. 'This could be a really important meeting.'

Mum wasn't having that, though, so we went over the big crossing and ran for a bus.

'Come on,' Ellen urged me, as Mum, Dad and Stephan found seats on the bottom deck. She meant for me to go upstairs with her and I did, Mabel clomping after us (clutching a Lego unicorn). I thought Ellen just wanted to discuss what we were going to do, but, once we were all sitting on the front two seats, she turned – and held out her dad's phone.

'Forgot to give it back,' she said, emphasising the 'forgot' to tell me that she hadn't forgotten at all.

'So call Whitecross House then!' I said.

The bus lurched off, pushing us back in our seats. Ellen found the number for Whitecross House and tapped it in. She put the phone on speaker and pretty soon an automatic voice was giving us loads of options. We were confused until it said,

'*To organise school or corporate visits, press seven.*'

'Press seven!' I shrieked.

Ellen did, and we waited. The phone rang for a long time and I thought there was no one there. But then a friendly voice said, 'Hello? Whitecross House. Sorry to keep you. Deborah James speaking.'

For a second neither Ellen nor I spoke. Then Ellen's eyes went wide and she grimaced at me. She held out the phone and flapped it up and down so I'd take it. I had no choice and before the woman – Deborah James – hung up I mumbled, 'Hello. My name is . . .'

'Yes?'

'Cymbeline Igloo,' I said.

'That's an interesting name.'

'Er, thank you.'

'And how can I help you, Cymbeline?'

'Well,' I said. 'Er . . .'

'Is it about a school visit?'

'Sort of,' I answered. 'More of a . . .'

'Yes?'

I took a breath. 'School project. We did go on a visit, but not to Whitecross House. We went to Hall Place, in London.'

'I've been there!' said Deborah James. 'Beautiful.'

'It is,' I agreed. 'And we saw this travelling exhibition of Elizabethan things. It's been to Whitecross House too.'

'It may well have done,' Deborah James said. 'We have a lot of visiting exhibitions. But . . . ?'

'And we saw something called the Phoenix Medal. It's a . . .'

Deborah James laughed. 'You don't need to tell me about that. The Phoenix Medal! It's world-famous. A marvellous piece, one of the best things we've ever had in the house. I haven't seen that for years.'

'*Years?*'

I didn't understand. We went to Whitecross House six months ago! Why would the burglars think that I had the Phoenix Medal if it hadn't been there then?

'You mean,' I said, 'it wasn't there recently?'

'Recently? No. I'd only just started here, I think.

Now when was it exactly? Hang on a second and I'll find out for you, Cymbeline.'

Ellen and I looked at each other, as Mabel stared at both of us. From the phone came the sound of a keyboard being tapped as Mabel asked what was going on. I was about to try and answer her when Deborah James came back on the line.

'Right,' she said. 'Got it. The Phoenix Medal was here at Whitecross House as part of our Travelling Tudors exhibition. Goodness, how time flies. That was in 2011.'

I thanked Deborah James and hung up. I was still staring out of the bus window.

'But that's ten years ago,' Ellen said – and my mouth dropped open.

TEN years ago?

I'm nearly ten.

And I went to Whitecross House when I was a baby.

Mum bought me Mr Fluffy there.

He was my first !Teddy of Most Extreme Importance! Mr Fluffy was my !Teddy of Most Extreme Importance! for nine years until I lost him – six months ago! At Whitecross House! I lost him in the river. But how could a baby (me) have taken the Phoenix Medal? It was impossible – and I still had NO idea why the burglars might think I'd taken it. It made NO sense at all – until a thought crashed through my brain.

'What is it?' Ellen asked, but I didn't answer. I just went through it.

I got Mr Fluffy from Whitecross House when I was tiny. And the burglars had attacked Veronique's teddies – but only the teddy teddies, not the other ones. And Veronique had been to Whitecross House too!

So – were the burglars looking for Mr Fluffy, not the Phoenix Medal?!

That HAD to be it! For some reason the Phoenix Medal and Mr Fluffy were connected, but how? I bit my lip and continued staring out of the window for inspiration, Mr Fluffy (who really was SO fluffy) flashing into my mind.

I saw him in my bedroom and on our kitchen table.

I saw him on the sofa as I watched a movie with Mum.

I saw him at school on Bring a Teddy Day, and then I saw him in the river, when I lost him, drifting right away from me, and then . . .

It was INCREDIBLE.

Because I didn't just see Mr Fluffy in my mind.

I was still staring out of the bus window. I wasn't taking anything in because of the thoughts spinning through my head – but my eyes were trying to focus on something. They were doing it on their own, almost without my knowledge. They took in the pavement below us, one stop before we were due to get off. They took in all the people looking in shop windows or heading towards the *Cutty Sark*.

Then they took in the girls.

There were two of them. One big and one small. Were they sisters? I didn't know, but I could see that they were holding something, swinging it between them like Mum and Dad had swung me at that brilliant time on the way to Hall Place. For a second I had an image of that too, before it disappeared.

CHAPTER FORTY-FIVE

Cymbeline

And I stared at Mr Fluffy.

CHAPTER FORTY-SIX

Jessica

The first people came on Thursday. Right after school.
They said they liked the living room and the garden.
Milly and I were silent. We just watched them, staring
around, looking like they were in some big shop
instead of OUR house. When they went up the stairs,
I fought the urge to shout out that they weren't
allowed in our room. Watching them go in was
terrible, though not as bad as watching the next lot
that came round later. They had kids with them. They
were boys, both a bit younger than us, and they ran
into our room and started shouting, one of them
getting told off by their dad for jumping on OUR
beds. That made me feel sick, but I didn't complain.
I didn't want to upset Mum, though she hardly said

anything. She left it to the estate-agent man, who sounded all bright and cheerful like this was some great, happy thing. When the people were leaving, they stopped in the drive and the parents told the estate agent that they'd definitely be in touch. I felt worse than TERRIBLE and I could see Mum's fists closing, her chipped fingernails digging hard into her hand.

On Friday three more sets of people came.

I tried to stay out of the way but, wherever I went, they showed up, and I had to keep moving. Milly said we should go to the park, but I shook my head. I wanted to be in our house for as long as I possibly could. I didn't even want to go to London on Saturday, though I had to of course because Mum was taking Dad to the hospital.

'Come on,' Mum said on Friday night. She must have seen that I was miserable. 'Let's just have a great day out tomorrow. Let's forget everything and have fun. It'll be great. And . . .'

'Yes?'

'Well, I haven't told you this, though you've probably guessed. It's not his fault that he's ill, but Dad feels so guilty. I know you're upset about the house and everything, but tomorrow, at least, can you try to pretend that you're having a nice time?'

I shook my head. 'No.'

'Jess! Come on. I know it's hard, but . . .'

'No. What I mean is . . .' I hesitated. 'I won't pretend. I will have a good time. It's not Dad's fault. We'll have a great day out in London, won't we?'

Mum laughed. 'If you count sitting in a hospital and then watching Brighton play Charlton! Go, Seagulls!'

'Can't we do something else as well?' Milly asked.

Mum said she'd think about it. She said she'd find out where Charlton was and see if there was anything interesting to do nearby.

'Now bedtime,' she said. 'Early start tomorrow.'

It was early. After breakfast, Mum pushed Dad down to the station in a wheelchair while Milly and I took turns pushing Benji. It was so weird seeing Dad in the wheelchair, but I didn't say anything. On the train it was better because he stood up and just sat down normally, though when we got to London we couldn't get on the Tube. We had to take a taxi to the hospital and I could see Mum and Dad glancing at the meter as the money ticked over, the ride getting more and more expensive.

'Mum,' I said, 'did you find somewhere to go near Charlton?' She nodded. 'Well, can we only go if it's free? There are lots of free things to do in London, aren't there?'

Mum dragged her eyes away from the meter and lifted her chin at me. 'Too late,' she said. 'I already bought the tickets online. Don't worry,' she added, before pulling me into a hug.

The hospital was right next to the River Thames. While Dad was being seen, Mum took us off for a walk and, in spite of the way I was feeling, it was pretty cool to be in London. We saw Big Ben, though it was covered in scaffolding, plus the Houses of Parliament. We saw a truck with people on, which drove straight into the water and became a boat. We also saw the London Eye, this big wheel with pods you can go in. We didn't, though, but I stared at it, watching it turn really slowly, thinking that it was just like life. It didn't stop. It just kept going, and you couldn't direct it. All you could do was trust, and hope, and pray that it would lead you where you wanted to go. I was going to say something about it to Mum, but she was looking at her phone. She nodded and I frowned.

'What is it?' I said.

Mum smiled. 'Would you like to go on a boat?'

'That one?' Milly asked, pointing at the boat that had been a truck.

'No. Different one. You can get a boat to where we're going, then it's just a short train ride to Charlton. What do you think?'

'Where are we going?' I asked.

The boat was a Thames Clipper. After Dad came out of the hospital we queued up. He warned us all about pickpockets, which he said London was rife with, and we crossed a gangplank to get on board. We stood outside, even though it was cold, and Mum pointed out landmarks as we cruised along. We saw Cleopatra's Needle, which Dad said would be useless for sewing with (groan). We saw Shakespeare's Globe and the Tate Modern, and then we stared up at the bottom of Tower Bridge. The boat sped up then, going *really* fast, all this spray flying up behind us. It stopped a few times and then we got off – at a place called Greenwich. I felt a bit wobbly on dry land, as if the whole world was moving beneath me, threatening to trip me up.

That felt like my life too.

The feeling didn't last long, though. It vanished as soon as we visited this museum overlooking the river. We actually went in because it had started raining, but it was really good. It had things from Henry VIII's Greenwich Palace in, like tiles from his chapel floor and these big cooking pots. I was glad about that because we were doing Henry VIII and I could tell Mr Newton, and I was also pleased because it WAS free. Though, when we came out, Mum said it wasn't all we were doing.

'We're going on that,' she said, pointing up through some trees.

What Mum meant was this MASSIVE wooden boat. To start with I thought that it must be in the river, but it wasn't. When we got closer, I saw that it was on land and the bottom had been encased in glass.

'It's like it's in an iceberg,' Milly said. And she was right. It looked amazing and I skipped forward, wondering what it would be like on board, though I still don't know.

Because this happened.

Mum looked at her watch. She said that we were a bit early for our time slot. That meant we could

341

have lunch so we went off to the left of the boat, which Dad said was called the *Cutty Sark*. We walked into something he called the Old Royal Naval College and found a bench. It had stopped raining now and it was all right to sit on after Mum had wiped it. Dad let Benji out of his pushchair for a runaround. Milly and I got our sandwiches out of my schoolbag – they were under Mr Goldy (no way we were leaving him behind). We took him out and, when we'd finished eating, I went to put him back – but Milly stopped me.

'Not fair,' she said. 'You want to see the *Cutty Sark* too, don't you, oh fluffy one?'

I nodded Mr Goldy's head for him, but then whisked him away. Benji had run up and tried to grab him.

'Nice try,' I said.

Milly strapped Benji into his pushchair and wagged her finger at him. 'You said "yuck", remember?'

Dad laughed. 'I did too. And that's really the smelly old thing you found in the river at Cuckmere?'

I covered Mr Goldy's ears. 'Don't listen to him,' I said, though it suddenly did seem really strange that he'd come all the way from there to here. He had a whole history from before he met us, didn't he, which we didn't know about? And, for the very first time, I pictured him floating along, twisting past ducks, turning through weeds and reeds and bits of old wood, sinking perhaps and then bobbing up again until he got to the place where we'd found him.

'Smelly!' Milly said, with a shake of her head. Then we packed up and walked on through the crowds towards the *Cutty Sark*, Milly and I holding Mr Goldy between us.

Until I felt something.

We were just coming out of the Old Royal Naval College, the road sweeping right towards the big boat. Milly was staring up at the tall masts, but I spun round because, all of a sudden, I was frightened. Why? I didn't know, and I scanned everything around me.

And saw a hand.

It was reaching through the crowd, but the mass of people was so dense that I couldn't make out its owner. All I could see was that it was reaching in *my* direction. It was almost on me and – thinking about the pickpockets Dad warned me against – I pressed my schoolbag into my side, ready to cling on to it. Without warning, though, the hand jerked back, probably because the group of tourists next to me had stopped to take photos. I sighed, and was about to tell Dad, to warn him too – but I felt it again.

This time it wasn't fear exactly. I just felt like something wasn't right. Something was happening, near me, something drawing me to it. I spun round, searching through the crowd, expecting it to be the hand again. There was no one very near me now, though, and anyway the feeling was coming from somewhere else, pulling my eyes to the side.

And up.

To a bus. It was a big red London one. I've never been on one and I wondered if that's why I'd spun round to it.

But it wasn't.

It was the boy.

On the top deck.

Banging on the bus window.

And shouting.

What he was shouting I didn't know because I couldn't hear – but he was in a frenzy. He was jumping up and down, which would have been enough to get my attention on its own.

But then I realised something.

The boy wasn't JUST banging on the window and shouting.

He was shouting at ME.

And then this happened.

CHAPTER FORTY-SEVEN

Cymbeline

Our eyes met. Mine and the small girl's. They locked on like laser beams – until the bus jolted forward. I stumbled, righted myself and looked again. But the girl had broken away from her sister and was trying to run through the crowd! And I couldn't help myself, the words bursting out of me like a Jack-in-the-box.

'MR FLUFFY!' I screamed.

I turned and leapt down the stairs, Ellen and Mabel galloping after, Ellen wanting to know what was going on.

'It's MR FLUFFY!' I screamed,

and the bus came to a halt.

'Cymbeline? Hey, Cymbeline! Cymbeline, wait!'

That was Mum, as we got to the bus stop. But I did NOT listen. Instead, I sprinted over to the door, waiting as it hissed open. Then I leapt on to the pavement, trying to stare through the forest of bodies and pushchairs, bikes and dogs, my brain spinning round like a washing machine: Mr Fluffy? Who I'd just been thinking of? Who was at the very centre of everything that was going on! Had I really seen him? The answer was YES, though that was totally impossible. How COULD he be there? I couldn't answer that so I just tried to find him – but where WAS he? All I could see were people: arms and legs and bodies and heads until . . .

'MR FLUFFY!' I screamed.

I'd spotted him. Half a leg and an arm – but it was him, up towards the *Cutty Sark*. Now I am usually an extremely polite person. I say please and thank you, and I ALWAYS hold doors open (and not just for women – sexist!). I also say 'excuse me' and I did

347

that now, as I smashed my way through the crowd.

'Excuse me!' I cried, as I bumped a girl off her skateboard.

'Excuse me!' I bellowed, as I grabbed a pushchair and spun it round.

'Excuse me!' I yelled, as I barged past two old ladies, one of their ice creams jumping out of its cone and taking off through the air like a tennis ball.

'Excuse me!' I roared, as I jumped over three chihuahuas and a guide dog, their leads getting tangled like spaghetti.

'Excuse me!' I shrieked, as I trod on the back of a nun's black dress and grabbed her arm.

What was *she* doing there?

And then it was wonderful. Then it was brilliant – because I saw him! And not just a bit of him. I saw ALL of my first **!Teddy of Most Extreme Importance!** He was up ahead, still with the two girls, though the little one was holding him now. She was clutching him to her chest and staring around – for me? I presumed so but, before she saw me, her eyes hit on something else and she gasped. And then she turned and ran – but I wasn't having that. She had Mr Fluffy so I chased after her, bobbing this way (**'Excuse me!'**) and that

('**Excuse me!**') until the girl was backed up against some wire railings, the river right behind her. There was nowhere for her to run now and so I sped up, then skidded to a halt in front of her.

And stared.

'That's my teddy!' I hollered.

'*Yours?*' The girl turned and stared at me. Some tourists did too.

'Yes,' I bellowed. 'That is Mr Fluffy!'

'No, it's not! It's Mr Goldy. Though . . .'

'WHAT?'

The girl thought about it. 'That's a really good name because he IS fluffy.'

'I know!' I screamed. 'He's VERY fluffy. He's Mr Fluffy and he's MINE!'

'No, he isn't!' spat a grown-up voice from behind me.

I didn't really take the voice in at first – I was too focused on Mr Fluffy. I strode forward, GLUED to my **!Teddy of Most Extreme Importance!**, and still SO amazed to see him. Though would the girl continue to deny that he was mine? I never found out because the owner of the adult voice leapt in front of me.

And it was the helper.

The helper from Hall Place! I gasped, sure that I'd

seen her before, and again trying to work out where. But, before I could, she leapt forward like a wolf – and grabbed Mr Fluffy!

'Stop!' the girl hissed, desperately trying to cling on to him. 'You lied. You said son and then you said grandson. AND you broke into our house!'

What?!

'SO LEAVE HIM ALONE!' the girl screamed.

But it was no use.

The woman was tall and too strong. With an almighty *W-R-E-N-C-H*, she tore Mr Fluffy out of the girl's hands and started to sprint away. But then I saw the other girl, who'd also been holding Mr Fluffy. The girl's sister? I had no idea but what I did know was that she was amazing. She crouched, leaned forward and FLUNG herself at the woman's legs. It was one of the best rugby tackles I'd EVER seen, though it only stopped the helper. It didn't knock her over. She did stumble, but she righted herself and shook the girl away, the girl trying to cling on. But she couldn't do it. The helper was too big. Soon the helper was free, a twisted delight flashing across her face as she started to move again, certain now that she'd escape.

But she was wrong.

CHAPTER FORTY-EIGHT

Cymbeline

Because she'd never met Mabel, had she?

CHAPTER FORTY-NINE

Cymbeline

I didn't even know that Mabel had followed me! But there she was, standing beside me – glaring at the helper.

'That is NOT your teddy!' she thundered. 'You're too old to have a teddy! That is Thimbeline's teddy!'

And then she did something fabulous. In a flash, her hand shot out, and all of a sudden a Lego unicorn (Uni-leg) was flying through the air. It was in fact the Queen of the Uni-legs, her long white horn spinning as she galloped – into the helper's face. This didn't stop her, though. It only startled her – but it gave Mabel time to prepare.

And then Mabel did what Mabel ALWAYS does.

She

!CHARGED!

Mabel piled into the helper's legs. It might have been that Mabel was smaller than the other girl, or just that no one can actually withstand one of her charges, but the helper went flying backwards. First she tripped on some steps and then she went crashing into the wire railings. And the result was great! The helper had flung a hand back on instinct, to protect herself. In it was Mr Fluffy and he shot high into the air, me whooping to see him free of the helper – until I saw where he was heading.

The Thames.

I'd lost Mr Fluffy once. In a river. SOMEHOW (and I had no idea how) that river had given him back – and brought him here. That river was just a normal river, though, and the Thames is HUGE. And fast. It's a giant grey monster and it was about to swallow Mr Fluffy – this time forever.

But then Ellen rushed forward.

She had been standing next to Mabel. She didn't charge, though. Instead, she ran carefully, her hands by her sides and one foot in front of the other – like she was doing gymnastics. And she was! First she did a cartwheel! That took her up to where the helper was sprawled out, and it was followed by a leap. That brought Ellen on to the top of the railings! They were wooden and wet – but she didn't fall. She simply ran along them until, one foot out in front, her leg almost parallel to the railings, she jumped!

And caught Mr Fluffy in mid-air!

Which was fabulous. Incredible! Ellen had saved Mr Fluffy from another river. But she hadn't saved him completely.

Because of the helper.

She was back on her feet now. And, when Ellen landed, she jumped forward – and there was nothing that Ellen could do. There was nothing I could do either – but watch as she tore Mr Fluffy out of Ellen's hand.

Though she didn't run away. Instead, she reached into her coat pocket and did something SO dreadful: she pulled out a knife! It was a Swiss Army knife and – after shoving Mr Fluffy between her knees – she picked out one of the blades. And then, too scared to approach her now, we just watched, in horror, as she jabbed the blade down into Mr Fluffy's stomach.

'No!' I screamed, and the two girls screamed it too. But it was no use.

The blade went in and the helper dragged it down, opening Mr Fluffy up. Once she'd done that, she shut the knife, shoved it back in her pocket and then dug her fingers deep into Mr Fluffy's chest.

And we all watched, wide-eyed, as she pulled out . . .

fluff.

And more fluff.

And then MORE fluff.

There was nothing else inside Mr Fluffy at all.

CHAPTER FIFTY

Cymbeline

I was STUNNED. I thought I'd worked it out! But the helper *wasn't* stunned. A flicker of angry disappointment flashed across her face – but then she nodded. She dropped Mr Fluffy to the floor, like he was NOTHING, and turned.

To look at ME.

The helper studied me, staring at my face to start with and then at my hands, and my clothes, studying me like she was seeing if I had anything else with me. And I realised that that was exactly what she WAS doing. And I also realised, in that moment, where I'd seen her before. And it was like a big hand had reached right inside me and squeezed my heart.

The helper nodded to herself. And then she ran.

She shot right past me and I ran too – towards Ellen. Somehow she'd managed her incredible gymnastics while still holding on to her dad's phone! I took it from her, then thrust it back, asking her to unlock it.

And I called Mum.

'Cymbeline!' she squealed. 'Where ARE YOU?'

'Safe,' I said. 'But you have to tell me.'

'Tell you what?'

'Where you bought Not Mr Fluffy!'

'Mr Fluffy? Cym, you know that.'

'No! Not MR Fluffy! I mean where did you buy NOT Mr Fluffy?!'

'The same place,' Mum said. 'We got him at the same time. We got him at Whitecross House.'

And I closed my eyes in despair. But then I opened them again, in time to see the helper running up through the middle of Greenwich.

Towards our house.

'Cymbeline!' Mum shouted. 'Now listen. Tell me where you are!'

'At home!' I screamed.

And I threw the phone back to Ellen and ran.

It's not far really. The bus might have been quicker, but I didn't know when one would come. So I sprinted up past the cinema and then the butcher's on Royal Hill. I pushed on past the bookshop and the fire station, and then I stopped at the zebra crossing until some cars had gone by. I walked over (YOU CAN'T RUN ON ZEBRA CROSSINGS!) and then sprinted as fast as I could towards home, nearly tripping as I barrelled down the alleyway that leads on to our street. At the end I stared at our door, before crossing the road and standing right outside it, which is when I realised – I DIDN'T HAVE A KEY! I couldn't get in!

But I HAD to get in! The helper was in there! She must have smashed a window or something because Mum was being careful now. But however she'd done it, I could hear her stamping down the stairs! And when I shoved the letterbox open I could see her too.

Holding Not Mr Fluffy!

And she was going to escape!

There was nothing I could do! In a flash, I knew why she'd asked Dad to bring me down to the *Cutty Sark*: she thought I might have Not Mr Fluffy with me. Now she was going to go out through the back door, just like she had when she'd burgled us! I banged on the door and screamed – but it was useless.

Until I heard footsteps pounding down the street behind me.

Dad? No – it was Stephan!

He sprinted towards me and collapsed against our front door. He was exhausted – but he didn't pause. Instead, he scrabbled around in his jeans for the keys. He pulled them out, but it seemed to take him ages to get both locks open because he wasn't that used to them. Eventually he managed it, though, and he shoved the door open, falling into the house with me darting in after him.

But we were too late.

A slam sounded from the kitchen. I chased in there to see the back door still shaking and a figure – the helper – ducking out into the garden.

With Not Mr Fluffy.

'No!' I screamed, but that just made the helper speed up. She rushed towards the fig tree, which she'd climbed before, knowing that she could do so again, in spite of the black dress she was wearing. And she was right. She was up the tree in seconds, the branches snapping beneath her feet, though that didn't stop her getting on to the garage roof.

But there was something the helper didn't know.

The helper didn't know about Stephan.

The helper didn't know that Stephan REALLY wanted to be a part of our family.

The helper didn't know that Stephan cared so much about my mum that he'd do anything for her.

The helper didn't know that this meant that he'd do anything for me too, that he'd think about my problems and work really hard to solve them for me.

Which meant that she didn't know about my ramp.

Rain. It's a pain, isn't it? It means you can't play outside sometimes, or your match gets cancelled because of a waterlogged pitch. Up until that day I'd hated rain, though I don't now: because, like some other things in life that may seem bad, it can help you to the best thing of all.

Which it did then.

The helper didn't see the ramp. Once on the roof, she just leapt forward, expecting to climb down the other side of the garage before running away. Without the rain she might have made it – but the ramp was slippery. Her legs started going fast, then even faster, until they were still going fast, but not on the ramp. They were going fast in the air. They shot right up while her head shot down, disappearing beneath the line of the garage roof. And then she was flying backwards, looping through the air, back towards our garden as I ran out. What I hadn't realised was that she'd let go of Not Mr Fluffy – and, while the helper crashed down on to our flowerbeds, my second **!Teddy of Most Extreme Importance!** sailed through the sky like Ellen had, flying right over my head.

Until Stephan caught him.

YES!

I grabbed Not Mr Fluffy from Stephan and pushed him into my face. I did it really hard, though not because I was SO pleased to see him (though I was). I did it until I could feel the lump, the hard lump, deep inside him, which sent a wash of relief flooding through me like the Thames.

Until a groan came from the flowerbeds.

I nodded. The helper was a bit hurt, but she was all right. Her big glasses had come off and I could really see it now – the resemblance. It was made even clearer when a horrified face peered over the garden fence.

And Mr Fells stared down at his sister.

CHAPTER FIFTY-ONE

Cymbeline
then
Jessica

The police cut Not Mr Fluffy open.

They did it on our kitchen table after arresting Mr Fells. And his sister. Mum was back by then with Ellen, Mabel and Dad, plus the two girls (Jess and Milly), their little brother and *their* mum and dad. Mum got the policewoman some scissors. Mabel held Not Mr Fluffy's hand, and told him to be brave, which he was. There was a snip, and then another snip. And there it was, little bits of fluff sticking to it but still unmistakable. The Phoenix Medal, with seven red roses and seven white ones, just as it should have had.

And that wasn't all.

The police pulled out a bunch of gold rings, some

jewels that looked like rubies, another necklace and three piano keys, one of which was worn down.

'The Middle C!' I exclaimed.

So they'd been fake too.

Mr Fells sighed, and his sister shook her head, and then the police led them both away.

'Who are you?' I said to the smaller girl, who I'd seen from the bus, holding Mr Fluffy.

Mum said that was a bit of a rude question, but the girl didn't mind. Neither did her parents. So she told me about living in Brighton, which is on the coast, and how they'd gone to this place called Cuckmere Haven.

'Benji did a poo,' Jessica said. 'We chased it.'

'You chased it?'

'That's right. Playing Pooh Sticks. You should have seen it go. When it stopped, we saw a teddy. It was muddy as MUDDY, and wet. Not like he is now.'

'Then why did you pick him up?' I asked.

'I don't really know. Maybe because he's special, and we could tell.'

I couldn't argue with that and I said so, before panicking. The helper had dropped Mr Fluffy on the ground near the *Cutty Sark*!

'It's okay!' Milly said, when she saw my face. And she held Mr Fluffy up for me to see.

Stephan called someone to come and fix our smashed bathroom window. Mum made a pot of tea. Jess's mum said they couldn't really stay because they were going to the Valley – to see Charlton play Brighton. Her dad laughed, though, and said they could skip it. He said that this was all far more important, and, while there isn't much that *is* more important than a Charlton match, I had to agree. The police wanted to speak to them anyway. They wanted to speak to all of us. We all had to give statements – and theirs were amazing. Apparently, Mr Fells's sister, calling herself Mrs Rose, had tried to con Jess and Milly into giving her Mr Fluffy! She'd also broken into their house to try and steal him.

'One of them must have seen you drop him in the river,' Dad said to me. 'At Whitecross House that time. After that, they must have been keeping a watch on social media to see if he turned up.'

Mum nodded. 'And then Mr Fells arrived next door. It was right after that, wasn't it? He must have found out who we were and moved here, not knowing which teddy the things were in. Yes?'

It sounded right, but Mum's question was properly answered an hour later. After we gave our statements, the police officers who'd taken Mr Fells and his sister off came back.

And they'd confessed.

'So what happened?' asked Jess and Milly's dad. 'I have to admit that I'm baffled.'

And what happened was this.

Mr Fells's sister had worked at Whitecross House for years. She was a helper, just like she then became at Hall Place. Whenever a travelling exhibition came, she took loads of pictures and gave them to her brother – Mr Fells – and he made incredibly detailed copies of them. When Mr Fells had finished the copies, his sister switched them with the real things. She then smuggled the real objects out of Whitecross House.

'In teddies?' I said.

The policewoman nodded. 'That's right. And one of them was Not Mr Fluffy, as you call him.'

'So how come my dad bought him? As well as Mr Fluffy?'

'Well, it seems that someone else working there saw Not Mr Fluffy and thought it was stock from the shop.

That's where Miss Fells had taken Not Mr Fluffy from in the first place. That person put him back, this all happening ten years ago of course.'

'And we bought him!' Dad said, putting his hand on Mum's arm. 'When Cym was a baby. The Fellses must have thought they'd lost their loot forever – because you had Not Mr Fluffy. But then we went back to Whitecross House and Miss Fells was still working there. She recognised us. But she didn't know whether it was Mr Fluffy, or Not Mr Fluffy, who you'd dropped in the river.'

'And this stuff's been inside Not Mr Fluffy all this time?' asked Mum.

'Yes,' I said. 'And, when Mr Fells burgled us, I had him at school, in my bag. Otherwise he'd have got him, and everything inside him. After that, he burgled Veronique's house, thinking he might find him there, while Miss Fells focused on Mr Fluffy in Brighton.'

'Right,' the policewoman said. 'And this morning she followed Jessica and Milly and family, from Brighton to Greenwich, looking for a chance to steal him. She also phoned your dad, Cymbeline, to get you lot down here and out of the way. When she realised that the medal wasn't inside Mr Fluffy, she rushed back here to break in again. But now do you want to see the rest of their stuff?'

We asked what she meant, but the policewoman just waved Mr Fells's keys at us and disappeared. Five minutes later, she was back. 'It's an absolute treasure trove,' she said. 'And all beautifully labelled. It's like the British Museum in there.'

She propped her phone on the table and showed us the film she'd just shot – in Mr Fells's house. There were coins: Greek, Roman and early British. There were small Greek statues. There were ancient turquoise beads and pieces of pottery. There was a pen used by Oliver Cromwell and a feather from Charles I's hat. And SO much more.

'He's got a whole workshop inside,' the policewoman said. 'Benches and hammers, drills and files. As for this lot, it's worth millions.'

'Millions?' said another policewoman. 'It's priceless. No wonder the Fellses went to all that trouble to get it back. First Mr Fells moving in next door. Then the burglaries. Then Miss Fells following Jessica and Milly from Brighton. And it was all nearly worth it. The other stuff will have earned them a pretty packet over the years, but the Phoenix Medal would have set them up for life!' She turned to Jess and Milly, and to Ellen and Mabel and me. 'And you lot saved it.'

They said the same at Whitecross House. That was two weeks later. It felt weird going back there again. It was great, though, as was the whole day. It started at school where Veronique and I were interviewed by all the newspapers and the TV stations about first seeing the Phoenix Medal at Hall Place.

'It was Cymbeline,' Veronique told the reporters. 'He said it was a fake. I didn't really believe him, I'm afraid. It was stupid of me. He was the one who saw it.'

I told them about going back there with Mum and Dad. Then we went up to our classroom where loads of photographers took our picture, the whole class getting in too, including Miss Phillips who went red, and Charles Dickens (who didn't). After that, I was allowed out of school early because Whitecross House is quite a long way away. Mum came to pick me up, but we didn't leave straight away. We had to wait, standing outside the gates, because Dad said he was coming to Whitecross House too.

And we waited.

And waited.

We stared up the empty road.

And waited some more.

And then Mum sighed, as I stared down at my shoes, nodding when Mum started to lead me off to the car.

But then I heard a shout.

'Sorry!' Dad bellowed, as he sprinted towards the gates.

And off we went, in Mum's car, me in the back while Mum drove, Dad making her laugh all the way.

And, when we got there, we saw the most amazing exhibition. It featured everything that had been found in the Fells's house – including the Phoenix Medal. We met Deborah James who told us that Miss Fells had worked there for years and they'd never suspected a thing. They even threw her a party when she left – to go and live closer to her brother.

'The Fellses must have taken something or other from every travelling exhibition that's been here for fifteen years,' she said. 'They sold quite a bit of it, to private collectors. That's what Mr Fells lived on. We're in the process of recovering it. But they kept a lot too. All this.'

'But why?'

Deborah James shrugged. 'History, I guess. To be around real things that really famous people touched in the past. It's a bit like a drug, I think.'

I frowned, remembering how Veronique had marvelled at those piano keys. I just couldn't understand it, until I thought of something that I owned, and about which I felt EXACTLY the same.

My Charlton shirt, which Jacky Chapman had actually *worn*.

'I get it,' I said. And then I turned away from Deborah James because someone was calling my name.

'Cymbeline!' Jess screamed.

And I ran towards him, wanting to tell him the news, which Mum had just told Milly and me. It was Dad. The hospital in London had found a treatment for him! It wouldn't make him better – he was going to have his disease forever. But the treatment would help him get through it. It would help him live his life as normally as possible.

'That's great!' Cymbeline said. 'That's fantastic.'

He wanted to know more, but we both had to be quiet. A woman was beginning to speak and what she said was almost as brilliant as hearing about Dad. She started with some boring stuff, thanking people for coming (Cymbeline did these snoring noises). She went on about all the 'artefacts', and how astonishing they were, though they weren't as astonishing as us – the kids who'd brought them all back. Everyone turned to Cymbeline, and Milly and me, the crowd clapping until the woman asked us to go to the front. We were each given a lifetime's membership to Whitecross House, and there was more clapping, and photos, and it was brilliant.

Though it wasn't the best thing.

Five minutes later, we were all standing around together – Cymbeline's family and ours. And this man came up. He started by saying how much he admired us, and we thanked him. But THEN he said what a great story it would make.

'Or, rather, it will make,' he said. 'If you let us make it.'

'What?' said Cymbeline's dad, suddenly looking very interested indeed. And the man explained. He worked, he said, for a TV company. A really big TV company. And they wanted to make a whole drama based on what had happened.

'If you let us, that is.'

'Let you?' Mum said.

'Yes. We'll need your consent. Both families. We'd have to buy the rights to the story from you.'

'For how much?' Mum said.

And the man took the grown-ups aside, all of us watching as, quite obviously, he told my parents, and Cymbeline's parents, how much money he was going to pay. Cymbeline's mum's eyebrows shot up. Her hand went to her mouth. My mum was equally shocked, though her reaction was different. She didn't look excited. Her face just crumpled. She bit her lip and then turned away. She held on to her stomach, folding over like she'd been punched. She fought for breath and then she started to cry. And cry.

Dad got to her, but he couldn't stop her crying. She just carried on, clenching and unclenching her hands, shaking her head when a waiter offered her a glass of wine in a tall glass. Then she started to thank everyone for having us. She hugged Deborah James and she hugged Cymbeline – and then told us that we had to go. Dad said that there was a party to come and that we hadn't really looked at the exhibition yet – but

Mum didn't care. She hurried us off to the car, leaning against it and crying again, before getting herself inside. Dad put Benji in and we drove home, Mum going a bit fast until Dad made her slow down. She did, sticking to the speed limit, though we could all tell that she was impatient, but that didn't stop her crying. Tears rolled down her face all the way home.

Mum slammed the brakes on. Then she jumped out of the car. She ran round the bonnet before stopping and running back. She got Dad's door open for him and helped him out, waving at us to hurry up and get out too, which we all did, Milly unstrapping Benji and me lifting him out.

And then Mum hurried us into the garden.

The front garden.

Where, with one MASSIVE yank, she pulled the For Sale sign out of the ground. She threw it on the grass and took Dad's hand in hers. In her other hand, she took Milly's. I grabbed Dad's hand, and then Benji's, and Benji took hold of Milly's.

To form a circle.

Of our family.

And then we all looked down at the For Sale sign. And jumped on it.

And jumped on it.

And we jumped on it, and we jumped on it.

And we **JUMPED** on it.

CHAPTER FIFTY-TWO

Cymbeline

And that's it. Or nearly. The worst of times followed by the best of times, just like I said at the start. Though, now I come to think of it, I didn't get that quite right. The worst of times was true but, actually, you can't ever have the best of times. That's just in fairy stories. The good that happens will always have some bad in it because, quite simply, you can't have everything.

Though I thought I could.

I thought I could work out who burgled our house.

And I did.

I thought I could work out how the Phoenix Medal had unequal roses one day and equal ones on another.

And I did. Mr Fells's sister realised that they'd been

sloppy and he painted one of the white roses red, not thinking I would ever visit Hall Place again.

I thought I could get Veronique back to being my best friend by showing how clever I was.

And I did, though not that way. She never stopped being my best friend. I just didn't realise. You see, friends move on, and grow, and just because someone has another friend it doesn't change how they feel about you. It just means your friendship has expanded to include someone else, or at least I hoped it meant that. I hoped that Veronique and I could be friends – but including Ellen too, who I now knew was fantastic. And not just for her gymnastics. Later that day she revealed that she actually really liked Subbuteo. She even had her own set of players – the England women's team – and she beat me six times out of ten. Halfway through, she asked if I wanted her to put on some music.

'No way!' I said, but Ellen laughed.

'Don't worry. Not the Squeaky Chicks. It's only Mabel who likes them.'

And she put on this band called Motörhead, who are just as loud as the Squeaky Chicks, but absolutely EXCELLENT (though Mum doesn't quite agree). All in all, I realised, now that we weren't fighting, that

Ellen was really cool, and I said this to Veronique. We were in the playground, at last play.

'But are you still going to see her?' Veronique asked.

I frowned. '*See* her?'

'And Mabel?'

'Of course. Why wouldn't I see them?'

'Well.' Veronique paused. 'It's just that your mum . . .'

'What about her?'

'Well.' Veronique winced. 'My mum and dad were talking. I heard them. And they said that your mum had a choice to make.'

'A choice?'

'Yes. I mean, she does, doesn't she?'

And, even though Veronique didn't say about what, I knew what she was referring to.

And I knew that she was right.

And I thought about that for the rest of the day, unable to concentrate on anything else. I saw Veronique again at home time and she looked sheepish, as though she shouldn't have said what she had. I didn't mind, though. It's why I like Veronique. She makes me face up to the truth of things. I said I was glad she'd said it, and that I had something to ask her.

'What do you think my mum *will* choose?'

Veronique shrugged. 'I've no idea. I think you'll . . .'

'Yes?'

'Just have to ask her.'

And I knew that Veronique was right. I nodded and she smiled at me, before we both went over to her mum, who was dropping me home that day. She chatted like she normally did, asking about our day, Veronique answering while I just sat quietly in the back, until we stopped outside my house.

'Thanks,' I said, as I shut the car door behind me.

And I took a deep breath, staring at our front door, wondering just how I could ask Mum what she was going to do. I also wondered when I could ask her, when I could get her on her own. The house was always so busy! How would she even hear me above the Squeaky Chicks?

But the house wasn't busy.

And there were no Squeaky Chicks.

Our front door was open, so I didn't have to knock. I just pushed it and walked in – and was stunned. As stunned as I'd been by the burglary. It was quiet – really quiet. And the hallway was . . . empty. Not completely empty, but the shoe rack only had Mum's shoes on, and my trainers. The coatrack was the same: no longer all humped over, but neat. Just our coats. Hers and mine. There was no toolbox underneath it. And, when I walked through to the living room, I stared at the sofa – back in the middle, not pushed up against the wall to make more space.

No.

And then I had a thought, and I spun round and ran up the stairs, though not to my room. I stood outside the boxroom, too scared to push the door open until I made myself.

And I saw that it was empty.

There were no mattresses on the floor. There were no leotards piled on the chest of drawers. And there was nothing hanging from the ceiling, or standing up on the shelves.

All of Mabel's unicorns were gone.

I took a breath. And then another. There was a burning at the back of my eyes. I walked backwards on to the landing, in a bit of a daze, until I heard talking from downstairs. Mum. I went to see who she was talking to and saw her on the phone, in the kitchen. She looked serious. And determined. I watched as she took deep, measured breaths, before she closed her eyes and shook her head.

'I'm sorry,' she said. 'But that's it. If you want to call us, you can. And you can come round too. I'd like that, though don't think that you have to. We had some very good times together and we can remember those. But that's enough. We don't need to pretend that us being together is something that should really happen. Because it isn't.'

Mum hesitated, and listened, until her face went all firm again.

'I'm sorry,' she said. 'But that's all I've got to say about it.' And, without waiting for an answer, she hung up.

Which is when she saw me.

Mum's eyes met mine. She walked forward and bent down to me. I thought she'd say something, but she didn't: she just used her thumbs to push my tears away. And then she did something odd, which she hadn't done for ages. I didn't even know that she could still lift me up, but she did it, stepping back to hitch me up as my arms went round her neck. I thought she wanted a hug – but she didn't. She started to move, me going backwards towards the front door and out of it. On the pavement Mum turned right, and I wondered where she was taking me.

I didn't have to wonder for long.

Mum went up to Mr Fells's door and tapped on it with her foot. What? Mr Fells was in prison. Everyone knew that. It was on the news.

But it wasn't Mr Fells who opened the door.

CHAPTER FIFTY-THREE

Cymbeline

It was Stephan.

'Cym!' he said. 'Good to see you. Well, come in then, you two.'

And in we went, into what was, Stephan soon told me, his new house!

'So you're going to be . . . ?'

'Living next door,' Mum said, setting me down on the floor.

'And you're . . . ?'

'Still together? Yes. Of course we are. It's just that you were right. Our place is too small for us all.'

'But what about the loft conversion?'

'We'll see about that. Meanwhile, Stephan's going to live here and do it up.'

'Sure am,' Stephan said. 'It's a right old mess. Your mum and I are buying it!'

'Really?'

'Really,' Mum said. 'And in a while we'll all move in together. Or we won't. Not everyone has to do things the same way. Families . . .'

'Families what?'

'Don't all have to look the same to *be* families, you know?'

And I did know. Certainly no other family looked like this one. But this family was great, and I was SO happy to be a part of it, in spite of missing Dad. Mum told me that he'd left.

'He got a part in that film. Six months in France. He went this morning.'

'Couldn't he have waited to say goodbye?'

'He didn't have time, Cym. Apparently. But he said to give you this.'

Mum handed me an envelope and I opened it. Inside was a piece of paper.

IOU one trip to see Barcelona at the Nou Camp, love Dad x

I folded it back up and put it in my pocket – which is when Ellen came in. She said she wanted to show me her new room and I was about to follow her – but I couldn't. Because, behind Ellen, was Mabel, whose eyes widened like stars.

'Thimbeline!' she screamed, before doing what Mabel ALWAYS does.

She charged.

Which really IS the end, apart from one last thing that you're going to have to help me with. We've got a problem and we STILL haven't solved it. Jess and Milly and I are friends now. Mum lets us talk on Zoom, and we're going to visit them in a few weeks because Charlton are away at Brighton (the first match was a draw). I REALLY like them both, and I know they like me – but we just CANNOT decide. I mean, they think it should be them and I think it should be me.

So what do you think?

Who should get Mr Fluffy?

He's not called Mr Goldy by the way. We've all agreed on that.

Mr Goldy is a RUBBISH name.

THE END

ACKNOWLEDGEMENTS

So, John Higgins, if you hadn't cooked us supper then Kate would never have said what she did and a certain very important person would have vanished forever. So thanks!

Thanks also to the wonderful Naomi Delap, for marrying me and being a great first reader. Writers can suffer from having too much time on their hands, so thanks to Franklin, Viola and Frieda Baron for making sure that that fate never befalls me. You're great. People ask me who Cymbeline is based on and I have to say he's an amalgam of lots of people I know (but thanks Rafe Griffiths).

Thanks also to Cathryn Summerhayes and the great team at Curtis Brown. Parties again soon, please.

Parties too, please, HarperCollins, because you are epic at them, as well as at employing the most wonderful editor in Nick Lake. And it's not just him. Samantha Stewart, Jane Tait, Jessica Dean, Jo-Anna Parkinson, Tanya Hougham and all the rest: you are Wonderful Things.

A final thanks to all the teachers and librarians who get in touch to tell me how much my books mean to the children who read them. You are essential beacons of light – for me, and for all writers for children.